IVAN
and the
daring escape

ivan
and the
daring
escape

MYRNA GRANT

Tyndale House
Publishers, Inc.
Wheaton, Illinois

For Stephen,
Elizabeth,
and Mary
—with love

Illustrated by
Jos. E. DeVelasco

Library of Congress
Catalog Card Number
76-8683
ISBN
0-8423-1847-X, paper
Copyright © 1976
by Tyndale House
Publishers, Inc.
Wheaton, Illinois

Second printing
November 1979

Printed in the
United States of America

contents

◆The threat of
the Secret Police

Ordinarily, Ivan loved the earliest days of spring. When other people were still complaining that winter was long and that it seemed spring would never come, Ivan would make the long journey on foot to the banks of the Moscow River. There, leaning over the great cement wall that edged the river as far as he could see, Ivan would smell the first fresh breeze of spring as it blew up from the melting ice on the river.

He always picked a spot where he could see the golden domes of the Kremlin churches gleaming in the pale sunlight across the river. How he loved Russia! There were times, standing by the river, that the desire to do something great and wonderful and beautiful almost overwhelmed him.

But today, watching the grey ice shift in

the dark straining waters, Ivan's heart was lead. Even the questions that had pounded inside his head for days were gone. Only the facts of the matter stuck in his mind.

Pastor Kachenko, one of the best and kindest Christian men Ivan had ever known, had been sent to a prison camp. There he would labor for three long years, convicted of a charge that was false. He had been sentenced as a parasite, a man who refused to labor in Soviet society, and who accepted money from other people rather than work. A most serious crime, if it were true. But everyone knew that all the pastors of Ivan's church had regular jobs in the many factories or mills that made Moscow the center of Soviet industry!

Ivan pried a piece of melting ice from the top of the cement barricade and threw it angrily into the river. Pastor Kachenko was his friend Pyotr's father. Soon Pyotr would meet him at the river. Ivan turned and leaned back against the river wall, and faced the street. Even though slush made the roads messy, cars and trucks were required by law to be clean in Russia's capital city. Ivan liked their shine and the sound of wet tires on the road. He

listened for a while, glad to have his attention diverted from his thoughts.

After a while he turned back to the river in misery. What could he say to his friend? Why did Pyotr so urgently want to see him? And again and again his thoughts kept returning to a strange and frightening incident that had followed the trial. After Pastor Kachenko's sentence was passed, there was an uproar in the courtroom. Believers protested, calling encouragement to Kachenko. Christians pressed forward to try to embrace him or give him flowers from the bunches they had smuggled into the room under their coats. Poppa wept. Ivan was pulled away from Poppa by the crowd. In all the press, he felt a strong tug on his sleeve. Alarmed, he recognized the face of the court secretary pushed up against his. Ivan had watched him throughout the trial, a tiny man whose round spectacles reflected the light whenever he raised his head. Recording, always recording lies about a good and loving man.

The secretary's face had been white with the terror of what he was doing. Violently he pushed a small packet of paper into Ivan's hands. His hoarse whisper was urgent.

"He was sentenced on false evidence.
You can protest."

Ivan had looked around him in panic.
But the confusion of the courtroom was so
great and the pushing of the crowd toward
Kachenko so determined that no one
seemed to notice.

Almost unwillingly, Ivan stuffed the
papers into his pocket. Someone knocked
the secretary's glasses partly off his face
and he grabbed wildly as he turned away.
Tears sparkled in his small eyes. In a
second he was lost in the crowd.

Dumbfounded, Ivan had given the papers
to Poppa when they were safely away
from the courthouse and walking home.
Poppa didn't even glance at them as he
took them. "The pastor will keep these
records," he had said sadly. "But they will
not help Brother Kachenko now."

"But why did that man give them to us?"
Ivan had whispered. "He was so afraid.
And someone could have seen him."

Poppa had nodded thoughtfully and
glanced over his shoulder before he
spoke. "It's likely that he's a secret
believer."

Ivan understood. He knew that many
people in Soviet society believed in Jesus

Christ but for reasons of their own they did not make their faith public. They did not attend church services or have friends among the Christians.

"There are many reasons for such people," Poppa always said. "We must not judge them. Their lives are very hard. Sometimes they come forward unexpectedly and help us very much."

Ivan pulled his mind back to the present. His eye caught a white water bird fluttering from one sluggish ice floe to another as if seeking a place of safety. It looked thin and frail. Anxiously, Ivan followed its progress. From time to time the wind lifted the bird and it floated effortlessly above the creaking ice.

Pyotr's voice startled Ivan. "Hello."

Ivan didn't look at his friend. "Hello, Pyotr."

Pyotr waited a moment, then thumped Ivan on the back. "Ivan, it's all right. Momma and Sonya and I are all right. You're a good friend to be so worried."

Ivan met Pyotr's eyes and gave him a grateful look. His friend's encouragement lifted his spirits. The last time he had seen Pyotr had been at the court when his father was sentenced. Pyotr, for all his fifteen years, had been weeping then, his eyelids swollen from lack of sleep.

"Sonya is just as usual. A three-year-old doesn't understand these things. Momma and I are thankful." Pyotr hesitated.

He put his hands in his pocket and took a deep breath, gazing out over the river. "But something more has happened. That's why I wanted to see you."

Ivan turned toward his friend in concern. Pyotr continued to look out at the frigid water swirling below the wall.

"The Secret Police are not content with sending my father away. They want my mother to denounce him."

"Denounce him? But Pyotr, what does that mean?"

Pyotr put a warning finger to his lips and answered quietly. "It means they want her to say that he was a bad man—that she agrees the trial and the sentence were just. That it is true that he would not work and help support the family. If she refuses, they say they will take Sonya and me away. They say we will have to be brought up in State boarding schools so we can learn how to be good citizens."

Ivan stared in horror at his friend.

There was a flapping of wings. The

river bird, lifted again by the wind, fluttered in front of them for an instant and then dipped toward the river. Suddenly Ivan smiled.

"But there is God!" Ivan was gripped with excitement. " 'Whoso dwells under the defense of the Most High shall abide under the shadow of the Almighty.' " Ivan repeated one of his favorite verses of Scripture as if he had never heard it before.

"Yes!" Pyotr grasped Ivan's hand and laughed. "He is the defense of the fatherless and widows. Oh, Ivan, how good it is to have a Christian friend!"

The two boys looked at each other happily.

"Come, Pyotr," Ivan said softly. "We will walk along the river and we will pray."

◆Pyotr disappears

"One-and-two-and-three-and-four! One-and-two-and-three-and-four!" A chill wind blew from the open window, flapping the curtains against the wall and lifting the pages of Momma's calendar. Katya's face was pink with effort and cold as she tried to keep up with Ivan in their morning exercises.

Ivan was freezing and wished he had not flung open the window as wide as it would go. Winter seemed to have returned but as long as Katya didn't complain, he wasn't going to be the one to close the window.

Faster and faster he counted until Katya began to gasp and laugh. Finally she collapsed into a chair.

"Ivan! You're going too fast! You can't ... exercise properly ... that quickly! What's the matter with you?"

Momma opened the bedroom door and

looked in. A great gust of wind raced through the room. Quickly she stepped inside.

"Goodness, children! It's cold in here!" She pushed the window shut and shivered, smoothing her hair. "Do you want to get sick?"

Ivan's "No!" exploded into the room with such energy, Momma laughed. *This is not the time to get sick,* Ivan was thinking. *I couldn't help Pyotr if I got sick.*

Katya reached for her sweater and pulled it on over her school blouse. "It's not so cold when you're exercising, Momma. It's only when you stop it feels chilly."

Momma gave each of the children a quick hug. "Breakfast is ready." She rubbed her hands together. "That will warm us all up. And hurry, please. We don't want to make Poppa wait."

Poppa's strong voice was always quiet when he prayed. Ivan loved this moment of the morning, when the four of them bowed together for the breakfast grace. Poppa was so full of praise to God. Even today when all of them were worried about Pyotr's family, the joy of Poppa's prayer encouraged them. Thanks for the food that day by day strengthened them. Thanks for God's presence that made them spiritually strong. Thanks for the gift of life, for salvation in Jesus Christ, for the opportunity day by day to serve Him.

When the prayer was finished Poppa smiled at Ivan as he took a thick slice of brown bread.

"Ivan, I know God is going to use you to help Pyotr. It takes real courage to keep going, day by day, in his circumstances. He needs your prayers and your friendship more than ever."

Ivan nodded and sipped his hot tea thoughtfully. "But Poppa, do you think it's true that the police would take Pyotr and Sonya away?"

Katya swallowed quickly. "I'd like to see anyone take Sonya anywhere! And if they did, they'd soon bring her back!"

The family laughed. The exploits of Pyotr's tiny sister were notorious. But the laughter died quickly and each face reflected the concern of Ivan's question.

Poppa answered slowly. "It is possible that charges could be made against Mrs. Kachenko that she is teaching religion to her children. That, as we know, is forbidden."

Momma closed her eyes for a second

and pressed her lips together. She took a deep breath and opened her eyes again. Her voice was steady and calm.

"Forbidden by the government. But commanded by God. I am sure the authorities know very well that all Christian parents teach their children about God."

Katya banged her empty milk glass on the table impatiently. "Then why do they pick on some people and not others? Why don't they just send everybody who is a Christian to a prison camp and be done with it? And this is supposed to be a free country!"

Momma put a firm hand on Katya's arm. "Katya, I have told you many times you must be careful what you say and what you think. Such thinking and talking will only lead you into trouble. You must learn quietness and patience."

Tears stung Katya's eyes. Poppa's voice was gentle in his reproof. "Katya, little one, your Momma is right. We must not be angry. And we must be grateful for the freedom we do have. Not so many years ago, all Christians *were* sent to prison camps, as you well know. It is not so bad as that now. And we are thankful."

Ivan cleared his throat. With a gasp, Momma glanced at the clock. "I must leave now or I'll be late for work!" Hurrying from the table, she pulled off her apron and lifted her coat from the hook by the front door of the apartment. "Katya and Ivan, please clear the table before you go to school." Her fingers flew down the row of buttons on her coat as she returned to the table for good-bye kisses. She gave Katya a special hug. "Work hard in school, children!" The children nodded. Poppa held up a hand in defense. "And I know, Natasha—I am *not* to work too hard at the factory. The children must work hard. I must not."

Momma gave Poppa an affectionate shake of her head. "You know what I mean. I'll see you all tonight." In a moment she was gone.

Ivan and Katya exchanged amused glances. Momma's "Work hard in school, children!" and her, "Don't work too hard!" to Poppa was a family joke. But Poppa did work hard at the factory anyway. He was one of the best workers. Ivan felt a surge of love for Poppa. He too could be taken away.

But Poppa was shrugging into his own

coat and pulling his cap on his head.
"Good-bye, children." He rumpled Ivan's
hair and pulled one of Katya's thick braids.
"Remember what Momma said." He gave
a warning look to Katya. Katya nodded.
"And Ivan, be all the help you can to
Pyotr today."

"I will, Poppa." There was nothing Ivan
wanted more.

After Poppa left, Ivan hurried to clear off
the table. In his mind he was planning
things to say to Pyotr. He could hardly
wait to get to school. Scripture that would
encourage Pyotr kept coming into his
mind.

What he didn't know was that already it
was too late.

◆Ivan investigates

The schoolyard was teeming with children. Most of them wore their dark winter coats swinging open in the cold sunshine of early spring. Splashes of red from the neck scarves of the Communist Young Pioneers gave color to the scene and cheeks pink from the still-present chill seemed to reflect the rosy color of the silk.

Ivan's eyes scanned the groups of children, looking for Pyotr's coat or collar without the red scarf. Christians did not join the atheistic Young Pioneers. Only Christians and students who were being punished were without the proud scarves. But in all the busy schoolyard, Pyotr was not to be seen.

All day long Ivan told himself that it was probable that Pyotr was at home ill. Or perhaps his mother needed him. It was very hard for his mother these days, and possibly Pyotr was shopping for his mother or helping with Sonya. Sonya was often sick in the severe Moscow winters and couldn't be taken to her nursery school. By the time the day was over, Ivan had convinced himself that Pyotr was staying home with Sonya so that his mother could go to work.

"Mara Kachenko's job will be more important than ever!" Poppa had said when Mr. Kachenko had been sent away to the labor camp. "She will be the only means of support for the family. It is possible she will have to try to find a smaller apartment."

"But their apartment is so small now," Momma had protested.

"All the same, the government gives no money to support the families of prisoners." Poppa's words trailed off in thought.

"And for us or anyone to help them, to give them money or food or clothes—it can't be true that this is a crime!" Ivan's voice had been shaking with indignation.

Now, hurrying home from school, Ivan's heart lifted. Naturally Pyotr was looking after Sonya for his mother. It was essential that she go to work. So engrossed was he in his thoughts Ivan had forgotten Katya.

"Ivan, wait for me!" Katya's braids were flying behind her as she ran to catch up. "Why didn't you wait? Have you seen Pyotr today? Is anything wrong?"

"Have *you* seen Pyotr?" Ivan stopped and waited hopefully as Katya caught her breath.

"No. I'm afraid the police have taken him away like they said they would." Katya's eyes were black with distress.

"Katya!" Ivan shook her angrily. "Don't talk like that! What a stupid thing to say!" Ivan turned and began walking furiously. He kept his eyes on the wet street. He could hear Katya's steps beside him, running to keep up. He didn't want to look at her, and apologize.

Suddenly he stopped and grabbed Katya's arm with delight. "Katya! I could go to Pyotr's to see if he's all right! I can get a bus across the street from our bus stop and just see what's kept him away today. It's probably nothing at all. And tell Momma I'll come straight home after I see him. I won't stay to visit. I won't even be late for supper."

Katya's grin assured Ivan that she

approved of the idea.

"Here, take my book. I won't be long."

Ivan sprinted away from Katya and across the road to Pyotr's bus stop just in time to jump on a crowded bus that was beginning to pull away. Gratefully he handed his *kopecks* to the person in front of him who passed the small coins forward to be given to the woman collecting fares at the front of the bus.

What a sensible idea, Ivan was thinking. He could imagine Pyotr's surprise when he opened the door.

A damp cold wind from the river had begun to blow when Ivan stepped off the bus. He buttoned his coat and shivered in the chill. The late afternoon sun had disappeared. Ivan pushed his hands deep inside his pockets and crossed the street to Pyotr's apartment building. A man leaning against the building bent his head to light a cigarette. Ivan shivered again. A premonition of danger fluttered in his chest. Ignoring it, he pulled open the heavy apartment door. The man gave Ivan an indifferent glance. It was only one flight of stairs to the second floor Kachenko apartment. Ivan walked slowly, listening. Was the building always this quiet? Was

something wrong? Fear seemed to hang in
the air.

As Ivan reached the second floor,
someone in the hall suddenly coughed.
Ivan froze on the last stair and looked
down the hall. Standing in the shadow of
the Kachenko door, a man coughed again
into his sleeve. Immediately Ivan
understood. The Kachenko apartment
was under guard. The man outside,
leaning against the building, the man
standing in the doorway, both were
KGB*, watching Pyotr's apartment! Ivan
must not be seen!

Quickly, his heart pounding, Ivan
continued to climb the stairs to the third
floor. It appeared that the man had not
seen him. Ivan could hear him now noisily
blowing his nose! "Thank you, Lord!
Thank you!" Ivan breathed. His mind
was racing. The men must not suspect he
had been coming to see Pyotr. But what
would he do on the third floor? How could
he appear to be making a natural exit from
the building?

Ivan gazed at the row of apartment doors
that lined the hall. He couldn't just stand
in the corridor. If someone came out of an
apartment, what would he say? But if he

*Secret Police

left too soon, would the officer waiting outside the building question him? Would he question him anyway?

Ivan walked softly to the end of the hall. A grimy window provided a depressing view of the wall of another building. Ivan pretended to peer out and tried to think. He wished Poppa were here. Poppa would know what to do. Ivan wondered what was going on inside the Kachenko apartment one floor below. He knew that in order to help Pyotr at all, he had to get safely out of the building.

◆Secret agents outwitted

It had been easier than Ivan expected. For some minutes he had waited in uncertainty, praying and wondering what to do. The sky outside the dirty window was darkening. Momma would begin to worry soon.

A noise in the silent hallway sharpened his senses. It was a door being unlocked. At the end of the hallway some small children came quietly out of an apartment followed by an old grandmother. She bent over the door lock, carefully trying the knob to make sure that the door was secure. Like a large dark bird, she huddled over the children, shepherding them noiselessly to the stairs. Ivan guessed that she had been caring for the children in her apartment while the mothers worked, and was now returning them home.

An idea flashed into Ivan's mind.

Quickly he walked to the stairs, smiling and raising his cap to the *babushka**. The old woman was startled, giving him a sharp look from under her kerchief which she wore pulled forward over her face. But Ivan smiled again. Keeping his voice low he smiled again in as friendly a manner as possible. "Let me help you, *babushka!*" Without waiting for an answer, he took the hand of one of the children. The woman proceeded slowly down the stairs. The secret policeman standing by the Kachenko apartment moved out into the middle of the hall and observed the small group descending the stairs. Satisfied, he leaned back into the shadows of the door.

Outside, the air seemed colder than ever. Ivan shivered violently and tried to talk to the small boy whose hand he grasped like iron. "Are you cold, little brother? Soon you will be with Momma, won't you?"

The child nodded gravely, observing Ivan with quiet surprise. The officer outside the building was still smoking. He stared at the group. Ivan wanted with all his heart to drop the small boy's hand and run. Instead he made himself keep pace with the old *babushka* who peered with

*Grandmother

23

fierce disapproval at the man. The agent had to think that Ivan had come to help with the children! Otherwise, as a stranger, he would be questioned.

As they passed the secret agent, Ivan could feel his eyes following them, but he made no move to stop them. At last they reached the end of the block and in a flood of elation Ivan turned the corner with the little group. He had been hoping against hope that the *babushka* would make a turn that would take them out of the view of the agent. Ivan released the little boy's hand and pulled on the old woman's coat. Patiently she stopped. *"Babushka,* grandmother, I must leave you. I must cross the road and get a bus home."

The grandmother nodded without interest. The small boy moved closer to her.

"Good-bye, grandmother." Ivan hesitated a moment then impulsively exclaimed softly, "Good-bye, and may God bless you!" The old woman raised her head, and gazed at Ivan, her face suddenly alight and knowing. She grasped Ivan's hand between her two mittened hands. *"Da! Da!* And you, my son. Yes! Yes!"

A surge of affection for her welled up inside Ivan. He smiled again. Tears reddened her old eyes. Quickly she gave him a smothering hug and nodding with happiness, she moved on down the street with the small children.

Katya and Momma were waiting anxiously as Ivan opened the apartment door. Momma hugged Ivan fiercely. "Ivan, I was so worried! What a foolish thing to do! To go all alone to the Kachenko apartment in times like this!"

"Is Pyotr all right, Ivan? Why wasn't he in school? Was Sonya sick?" Katya threw the questions at Ivan excitedly.

"Katya, let Ivan get his breath! Look how cold he is! Ivan, you must have some tea and warm up." Momma moved into the small kitchen calling instructions over her shoulder. "You just sit down, Ivan, and don't say one thing until I bring the tea. It's all ready."

Ivan sank gratefully on the couch. In the familiar yellow glow of the parlor lamp, safe at home, the tension of the past hour seemed distant.

Momma poured the amber tea into a

glass and handed it to Ivan. Katya perched on the arm of the sofa in expectation. She could tell something had happened.

When Ivan finished his story, Momma looked very grave. Slowly she searched for reasons. "I do not understand. Pyotr not in school. Two secret agents guarding the apartment. Why should a lone woman and two children require a guard? I do not understand."

Katya swung her legs and bit her lip thoughtfully before she spoke. "Could they have arrested Mrs. Kachenko? Do you think Sonya and Pyotr are all alone?"

Momma got up and put her arms around Katya. "Oh, no, Katushka! They wouldn't leave children alone like that...." But Momma's voice trailed off in bewilderment.

Katya pulled away from Momma and took a deep breath. Ivan admired her courage. He knew how much she wanted to give in to the fear that pulled at all of them.

"I'm hungry, Momma."

Ivan grinned. He knew food was the last thing Katya wanted.

Momma smiled. "Yes. Poppa will be

home anytime, and we are not ready for supper." Momma tied her apron in a firm bow. "I'll heat up the soup while you set the table. Poppa will know what to do."

Poppa had laughed in delight at Ivan's story of the escape from the building. Ivan loved the way Poppa could find something funny in almost every situation. "That poor little boy is probably still wondering who the big brother was who took his hand!" Everyone at the table had smiled at Poppa's mirth. Just having him home made them all feel better. And hearing him laugh seemed to make the situation far less serious.

But Poppa had not known what to do. For him or any of the pastors to go to the Kachenko apartment would be useless. Not only were they sure to be refused admission, they would bring themselves under suspicion. "Of course there is an explanation." Poppa had spoken cheerfully, smiling at their worried faces.

It seemed Poppa was not terribly concerned. But after the meal was cleared away, Poppa put on his coat. "I'm going to tell the pastors what has happened," he explained. "We must pray and ask God what to do." Unexpectedly he turned to Ivan. "Son, would you like to come with me?" Mystified, Ivan agreed. Momma's face paled slightly but she said nothing. Katya looked jealous.

"I want to come, too, Poppa! Please, let me come!"

Momma pulled a braid playfully. "And leave your Momma all alone? Certainly not! And besides, you have homework to do."

Katya opened her mouth to say Ivan had homework, too, but Poppa stopped her with a raised finger.

"You pray with Momma at home!" he ordered. "And then go to bed. We won't be long."

But the look that Ivan saw Poppa give Momma meant just the opposite. It was a look that said, "We might be very long indeed."

◆The plan

The most essential thing, all the pastors had finally agreed, was to make contact with Mrs. Kachenko. "If only she had a telephone!" Poppa had smiled wryly. "That would make it so simple!" The pastors had smiled, too. None of them had such a luxury, either. Problems were not settled so easily in the Soviet Union.

"But it's not possible to visit her," Ivan reminded the men. "Even in the afternoon there were two secret police guarding her apartment. At night there might be even more."

"If not more, it is true the watch will be kept." Pastor Aranovich gazed thoughtfully at Ivan. "But we must find out what has occurred. We cannot leave our Christian sister without comfort and help."

Sitting in the circle of men in Pastor

Aranovich's comfortable living room, Ivan felt part of the grown-up world. It was strange to be out so late at night and to be included in the hushed prayers and discussions concerning Pyotr and his mother and little sister. Ivan wondered how many similar meetings Poppa had attended before. Meetings that Katya and Ivan had not known about. It was true that for Christians meeting together at night was dangerous. If they were found out there would be questions at the police station. It would not be enough to say they were a group of friends enjoying each other's company. The police were certain to suspect that something illegal was being planned.

Always the laws to make life difficult! Sometimes the unfairness of it made Ivan impatient and fearful. If only there were not such laws. If only God would change the hearts of the men in government and there would be a declaration that laws against Christians were abolished!

"Ivan, Ivan!" Poppa always scolded Ivan playfully when he said such things. "The New Testament tells us that we shall be persecuted and put in prison. We are told also to be joyful when we have trials, not to wish that they be taken away. You know what the Scriptures say!"

But it was hard to take comfort in those Scriptures when your friend had disappeared and his apartment was being watched by the Secret Police.

Ivan was growing sleepy in the long discussion. His attention strayed. Pastor Aranovich had a piano. Ivan studied it with interest. No one else he knew owned such an instrument. But Pastor Aranovich had an unusually good job. He took class photographs of children in the Moscow schools. He was so good at his job that his supervisor didn't care that he was a Christian. All the believers were proud of him.

The top of the piano was covered with a heavy cloth and dotted with small figurines and family photographs. Ivan had never seen so many. On one end was a cuckoo clock given to Pastor Aranovich by some relatives in another country. It was the most unusual clock Ivan had ever seen. He was fascinated by the cuckoo popping out of the tiny window, and the little carved balcony under the window.

Suddenly Ivan had an idea. "Poppa!" He burst out so loudly the men looked at him in astonishment. Poppa quickly put a finger to his lips and frowned in warning. Ivan nodded and quieted his voice although the words poured out in excited whispers.

"I know another way into Pyotr's apartment! At the back of the building are balconies. Every apartment has a little balcony. One day Pyotr forgot his key and he told me how he climbed up the balcony and got in!"

"Just a minute, Ivan. Slow down." Poppa's face was alive with interest. Ivan saw him look questioningly at the pastors. Pastor Aranovich nodded for Ivan to continue.

"Pyotr keeps a thin stone on the top of the window ledge. The windows slide open sideways. With the stone he can push back the lock and open the window. As long as the police aren't watching the back of the building I know I can get in."

Several of the pastors looked doubtful. There was a buzz of conversation. "It's too dangerous for a boy..." "What if police are watching the back of the building?" "Someone would have to go with him..." "No, a man would be arrested for breaking into an apartment... It would be too difficult for a man..." "It's too dangerous for a boy!"

One of the older pastors raised his voice slightly. "It is too dangerous, I say. We'll have to think of something else."

Ivan felt as if a door had slammed in his face. He wanted to argue, to pound at the door. But Poppa gave him a quiet look and Ivan tried to control his disappointment. There was a long silence in the room as the men thought.

Finally Pastor Aranovich spoke. "There is no question that it is dangerous. But even if Ivan is caught, perhaps the police will think it was simply a schoolboy attempt to see his friend. Of course, there will be trouble about it. But perhaps the trouble will not be too bad."

"I won't be caught!" Ivan insisted eagerly. "If I see that the back of the building is being watched I'll just come home. And if it is all clear, I can be inside the apartment in a minute."

Poppa rumpled Ivan's head in affection. "Of course, you may scare Mrs. Kachenko to death. That's a problem, you know."

Ivan's mind was racing ahead. "I won't scare her. When I get the window open, I'll whistle a hymn. She'll know it's a friend."

There was a stir of agreement around the circle. It seemed to be the only way. But the evening was wearing on. If it were to be done, it would have to be quickly. It wouldn't do for Ivan to be seen on the streets too late at night.

In spite of the need for haste, the men bowed again in prayer. Voices rose and fell, committing Ivan to God's care, asking for guidance as they made plans.

Ivan's heart was pounding in excitement.

◆Sudden fear

Poppa and Ivan hadn't talked on the bus ride to Pyotr's neighborhood. For one thing, the bus was almost empty and any conversation would have been overheard by the weary-looking conductress who swayed against the side of the bus as the vehicle made its way slowly through the dark streets.

For another thing, Poppa's eyes were closed. Ivan knew he was praying. Ivan tried to pray too, but he was so excited he couldn't concentrate. His eyes kept flying open to make sure they hadn't gone past their stop.

Ivan tried to remember what he was to say if he were caught. Caught! The thought stung him with fear. He took a deep breath, biting his lips and dispelling the thought. He took another deep breath. He would say his friend was not in school and he wanted to know why. He was afraid of the man standing in the door. Of course it would mean a trip to the police station and questioning. "You won't be afraid of that, Ivan, will you?" Poppa had looked anxiously into his son's eyes. Interrogations were not to be taken lightly. Sometimes they lasted for several hours, even all night.

"No, Poppa. That is nothing compared to the difficulties the Kachenkos are having. I won't be afraid. And besides, I will be telling the truth."

Poppa pulled on Ivan's sleeve and began to get up. Ivan slid out of his seat quickly and lurched toward the door, Poppa following closely behind. There was a grinding of brakes as the bus door opened and the Nazaroffs jumped out. Ivan shivered violently in the night air.

It had been decided that Ivan would go alone to the apartment building and Poppa would wait for him at the bus stop. Transportation was very slow in the evening hours. It was unlikely that another bus would come by for at least an hour, so Poppa would have a good waiting place. Ivan nodded silently to Poppa and turned toward Pyotr's building, squaring

his shoulders and walking as fast as he
dared.

His footsteps seemed to echo loudly
down the street. Ivan tried to walk on
the balls of his feet, hardly letting his heels
touch the sidewalk. A wind rattled the
bare branches of the trees that grew along
the parkway, casting vast spidery shadows
on the sides of the buildings as Ivan
passed. His heart pounded as he turned the
corner to approach Pyotr's building from
behind. His eyes scanned the street as far as
he could see in all directions. It was
deserted. Thankfully, Ivan cut across a
bit of lawn to the tall hedge that
surrounded the apartment property. With
a gasp of dismay, Ivan stood still. Behind the
hedge was a steel mesh fence!

Desperately, Ivan stood back from the
secrecy of the hedge and looked for a
break in the foliage that would signal a
door. There was none. Pyotr hadn't told him
about the fence! Grasping the fence
above his head, Ivan pulled himself up,
trying to wedge a toe into the small,
slippery openings of the meshwork.
Immediately his foot slipped, pulling his
body downward with a violent lurch. Ivan
clung to the fence with all his strength

and tried again. His hands were burning
from the pull on the ice-cold metal, but by
heaving himself upward and pushing rapidly
with his feet he reached the top of the
fence. With a mighty heave, Ivan thrust
himself over the fence and dropped to the
ground.

His heart was racing madly and he
remained crouching by the fence,
listening and looking. All was silence.
Somewhere in the distance a dog barked.

A dog! That was something they hadn't
thought of. What if someone owned a dog
and it began to bark? Ivan shuddered.
"Lord, don't let there be any dogs here.
Or, if there are, please keep them quiet."

Cautiously Ivan raised himself and
searched the long yard for signs of danger. A
young moon glimmered dimly in the
misty sky, hardly giving enough light to
make shadows on the cold ground. In a
wild spurt of speed, Ivan raced across the
yard and flung himself over the low balcony
below Pyotr's floor.

The blinds were drawn across the first
floor apartment windows. In alarm, Ivan
could hear a radio playing and a man's
voice talking through the thin walls.
Carefully, Ivan climbed up onto the

railing of the side of the balcony and
leaned against the apartment wall. Above
his head was the Kachenko balcony. By
standing on his toes, Ivan could just reach a
small ledge that was raised along the floor
of the balcony. With a tremendous
effort, Ivan hooked his fingers over it and
pulled himself up. It was much harder
than Pyotr had said. With a gasp of relief,
Ivan rolled his body over the Kachenko
railing and huddled under the window.
The blinds in Pyotr's apartment were
pulled down, also. But a rod of golden
light shone out from under the lower edge
of the shade at the bottom of the window.

On the street Ivan could hear rapid
footsteps. Anxiously he crawled to the
railing and narrowed his eyes, straining to
see. An old man in a long coat was being
pulled along by a tiny dog. Ivan grinned in
relief and cautiously stood up, keeping
his body close to the wall and in the
shadow. Slowly he raised his arm to the
top of the window and felt along the ledge
for Pyotr's sharp stone. Immediately he
found it. It was almost as if he could hear
Pyotr giving him directions.

"I just stuck it in where the window
locks and pushed the lock back with it. It

was simple."

The window slid open easily. Gently Ivan pushed the long blind back and put a leg into the room. A thought suddenly struck him in terror. What if the KGB were inside the apartment? For an instant Ivan froze. Then, picturing how he looked with one leg on the balcony and one inside the apartment, he gave a small laugh. He had come too far to run away now! Softly he began to whistle an old Russian hymn. Steadying himself, he swung the other leg into the room and ducked under the blind into the blazing light of the Kachenko parlor.

◆The night visit

"Ivan!" Mrs. Kachenko was standing in the middle of the room staring with terror-stricken eyes at the window. Her face was as white as paper. Weakly she sank into a chair, shaking violently.

"Oh, Ivan, how glad I am to see you!" Mrs. Kachenko held out her arms to Ivan and hugged him. Tears began to stream down her face.

Ivan glanced around the tiny room for the radio. Seeing it on a small table by the front door, he gently pulled away from Mrs. Kachenko and turned it on. Vigorous Russian folk music filled the room.

Ivan pulled a straight chair toward Pyotr's mother, and sat down. "I haven't much time," Ivan began. "Poppa is waiting for me outside. The pastors are concerned about you because of the police guard around your apartment. And where is Pyotr?"

Mrs. Kachenko grasped Ivan's hand urgently. Ivan could see she was trying to compose herself. She had stopped crying, but her voice trembled.

"Ivan, tell the pastors that the police want me to denounce my husband. They want me to say he was a bad man and made life hard for me and the children. That he wouldn't work and provide for us." Tears again poured down her face.

Ivan's face tightened in anger. Mr. Kachenko had worked long hours in an auto factory. But Ivan said nothing. He fought down his feelings.

Mrs. Kachenko lowered her voice even more, although the music played on.

"Of course, I refused to do such a thing. Then the police became very angry. They said I was an unfit mother and unless I denounced my husband, they would take away my children. I do not understand why it is so important to them that I should tell such lies. They already have my husband."

Ivan's anger vanished in a stab of fear. "They have taken away Pyotr and Sonya?"

"Sonya is here. Sleeping." Mrs.

Kachenko nodded toward the apartment's one bedroom where a dim light burned. She cleared her throat and pressed her lips together. Tears again flooded her eyes. She tried to speak but shook her head helplessly. "They have taken Pyotr away?" Ivan repeated.

Mrs. Kachenko nodded. Her voice had become thick with crying. Ivan strained to hear her. Happy music filled the room.

"He left for school this morning as usual. But he did not come home. Instead, two Secret Police came. They told me Pyotr was safe and I would see him when I denounced my dear Georgi. They told me Sonya would be the next to go."

Ivan held up his hand in warning as he heard a step at the door. The police agent outside had begun pacing back and forth in front of the door. Mrs. Kachenko's voice was even lower than before. "They won't let me out of the apartment, Ivan, because they know I would tell our believers what has happened. They think by making me stay in here, all alone and without Pyotr, I will change my mind."

Ivan pressed Mrs. Kachenko's arm awkwardly. "I will tell the pastors. They will know what to do."

Mrs. Kachenko leaned her head against the chair. "They do not understand that I will never say Georgi is a bad man. They think I am alone... But, Ivan, God is with me. He is my strength. How close he is to me!" Mrs. Kachenko gave Ivan a fleeting smile. "But I must know if Pyotr is all right. I must know where he is. Oh, Ivan, tell the pastors I want my son back!"

Ivan nodded. Quickly he bowed his head. "Blessed God of Heaven, our Father and Lord, give Mrs. Kachenko all the strength she needs right now. Help her to know she is not alone. Protect her and give her your wisdom. Protect Sonya and Pyotr. In Jesus' name, Amen."

Mrs. Kachenko raised her head and gave Ivan a second smile. "What a good boy you are, Ivan." She patted his hand. "You must go quickly. But don't fear! There is only one officer guarding at night. Out there!" She motioned with her thumb toward the sound of the footsteps at the hall door.

Ivan nodded. Pyotr's mother squeezed Ivan in a swift hug. "Hurry now! God go with you!"

In a moment Ivan was outside the window and moments later on the street, breathlessly making his way to where **his** father would be waiting. With tremendous relief, he turned the corner and saw Poppa's figure, small in the distance, huddled against the cold at the bus stop. Ivan waved silently. The figure seemed to stare for a moment, then wave enthusiastically. Ivan grinned. How good it was to see Poppa!

◆Ivan's mistake

The police official, Comrade Jarmansky, had unruly black hair and eyes that flashed in cool amusement. He gazed at the small group of pastors in his office, his eyes resting on Poppa and Ivan. He had a large stomach that hung over his belt and Ivan watched in fascination as it began to shake in forced laughter as he stood before them.

"But it is too absurd!" he finally gasped. "What a silly story for grown men to tell me: that our great Moscow security department has nothing better to do than snatch boys from their mothers! Impossible! Even you admit that there were no charges against the mother, and no trial. Such a thing is not done in our modern socialist state."

Ivan glanced at his father standing with the pastors in the room. Ivan was surprised that all the men were calm. That they were not angry at Comrade Jarmansky's lies. Poppa was the spokesman. Because he was not a pastor it was less dangerous for him to speak.

His voice was quiet and insistent. "But all the same, Comrade officer, it has been done. The boy is gone."

Jarmansky had stopped laughing but an unpleasant smile lingered on his face. He glanced at Ivan.

"At such an age, some boys wish a little adventure. It is unfortunate but true that some boys run away from home for a few days. I have young Kachenko's school record. He was a poor student. He did not belong to the Young Pioneers. He was somewhat maladjusted. If he is not at home it is possible that he has chosen to run away and frighten his mother for a few days." He yawned in unconcern.

"He was a good student!" Ivan burst out. "His marks were very high! That record is wrong if it says he was a poor student. And Pyotr would never run away."

The smile instantly vanished from the officer's face. Poppa laid a hand on Ivan's shoulder.

"My son is worried about his friend. I hope you will pardon the outburst of a child."

Comrade Jarmansky continued to look offended. Ivan's face flushed. He knew it was always unwise to argue with the police, no matter what was said.

Now the officer's voice was grave. "There *is* indication that Mrs. Kachenko is an unfit mother. If this is so, she will be charged. If she is found guilty, that is the time to remove children from harmful parental influences. But such an unfortunate necessity does not take place without a proper trial."

Remembering Mrs. Kachenko's words about how the agents had openly admitted taking Pyotr, Ivan was stung with the officer's hypocrisy.

But Poppa nodded respectfully. "We know this woman to be a good mother, Comrade. If there is such a trial we would be eager to tell what we know of her to the court."

The officer's eyes narrowed and he sat heavily at his desk. "If you have influence with her it would be well if you could persuade her to denounce her husband. By her refusal she is showing rebellion against our Soviet reality. Such a person is not fit to raise children."

There was silence in the room. A dreadful feeling of despair settled over Ivan. The iron machinery of the state was in motion. Who could escape it? Already it seemed to have devoured Mr. Kachenko. Pyotr was in its grasp. Now it was moving ever onward, reaching out for Sonya and Mrs. Kachenko.

A small bird lit on the windowsill of the officer's half-opened window. Ivan moved his gaze to the bird and stared dully at it. It rested a moment, then was gone in a wingflash. Unexpectedly Ivan spoke, almost shocked by the angry sound of his own voice.

"You are saying that a person who will not lie is not fit to raise children!" His indignation cut into the quiet like an electric shock. Poppa moved slightly toward Ivan, but Ivan ignored him.

"You yourself have said nothing but lies this whole time we have been in your office! You know very well what we know: that Pyotr was taken away by some of your own KGB men. You know it is not legal and that you do this to frighten his mother."

A red spot began to appear on each of the officer's cheeks. Ivan watched them spread over his whole face as he listened. But Ivan couldn't stop, even though Poppa's hand was now on his arm and Poppa was telling him to be silent.

"All we want is for Pyotr to be returned home. But how can we ask you when all you say is that you have not taken him and that he has run away? It is a lie. All you have said is a lie."

Jarmansky was shaking violently. He had stood to his feet and only sputtering noises came out of his mouth. His eyes were twitching with fury. Finally he found his voice.

"You! You dare to speak like this!" The officer swung toward Poppa, whose hand was now tightly clamped on Ivan's mouth. "This is an example of how you teach your child? This is what you permit?"

"I do not permit it!" Poppa's voice was strong. "Such conduct is uncultured and I most sincerely apologize, Comrade. Please, my son is not himself. He is sick with worry..." Poppa released his hand.

"You people think you know so much! You understand so little. You understand nothing of our glorious Soviet reality and how quickly the great goals of the Revolution can be twisted by people who wish to do us harm!" The officer's voice was hoarse and choked with rage. "It is not only within that there are dangers ... but also without! Those outside who would slander..." Suddenly the officer stopped in alarm.

All of Ivan's emotion had drained away. He stood fearfully beside his father, staring at Comrade Jarmansky.

Poppa nudged Ivan. Ivan cleared his throat. "I apologize, Comrade, for my bad conduct..."

"Get out!" The officer was wiping his flushed face with a handkerchief. "Get out and do not come back! All of you!" The officer held up a warning finger to Poppa. "If I see that son of yours, Nazaroff, if I ever see him again, I myself will arrest him!"

Ivan's knees were still shaking as they made their way to the street. Such a shame filled Ivan he could not look at Poppa or the pastors. *I've only made it worse. I've made it worse!* The self-accusal stabbed at him over and over as they walked.

At the corner of the long boulevard was the famous Moscow children's theatre.

Above its doorway had been constructed a huge and wonderful clock. Children came from all over Moscow, and tourists from all over the world to see it strike the hour. Poppa broke the depressed silence of the group. He put his arm around Ivan, "Look, Ivan! The clock! It's going to chime!"

Ivan was astonished that his father could point out the clock. He glanced up to see comfort in his Father's eyes. Tears stung his own.

"It's eleven o'clock." Poppa pulled Ivan toward the clock and the small crowd watching it. With a nod, the pastors continued on their way.

"First comes the dancing bear!" A chime struck, followed by a playful tune. A door in the clock swung open and a large stone bear, clumsily turning and nodding, delighted the crowd. Poppa's voice was husky. "I think the rooster is next." Again Poppa put his hand lightly on Ivan's shoulder. A second chime momentarily interrupted the music and the rooster's door was opened. A cat on a huge golden chain sprang out from behind another huge door and joined the colorful dance. Children in the crowd laughed and applauded as toy after toy performed, each on its own revolving stage.

Ivan turned away, his head lowered. In
the midst of the music and the merriment,
he was crying.

◆The lurking stranger

The morning air was so warm Katya had flung open all the windows of the apartment and was joyfully twirling and leaping about the rooms. Her long brown hair, not yet braided, flew about her head in a cascade of motion.

Ivan, buttoning his shirt in his bedroom doorway, stared at his sister in disapproval.

Poppa put down his coffee cup in mild surprise. Momma shook her head helplessly.

"I'm going to be happy! I'm going to be happy!" Katya jumped up on the couch and leaped down again too quickly for Momma to do anything except open her mouth in protest.

"Happy!" Katya spun past Ivan. "Happy!" She gave Poppa a kiss on the top of his head. "Happy!" She swung away from the hairbrush in Momma's hand.

"Today we are having a puppet show in school. Today it is spring! Today is one day closer to Easter! Today I shall wear pink ribbons!" Katya bent grandly, like a ballerina, and with both hands pulled open the bottom drawer of the chest in which Momma kept her ribbons. With a flourish, she handed them to Momma and plopped down on a chair beside her.

"Momma, you ought to do something about Katya!" Ivan twisted his tie into position and took his seat at the table. "She's old enough to understand about the Kachenkos perfectly well, yet she behaves in this unfeeling manner."

Poppa smiled gently. "Ivan, we all need a change. I think that's what Katya is saying."

Momma was brushing Katya's hair vigorously. "It is true we have been worried and depressed a very long time. We have prayed much about Pyotr. Perhaps now it is time to forget our mistakes and to believe that God will answer our prayers."

Katya twisted in her chair and gave her mother a dazzling smile. "Oh, yes, Momma. I woke up this morning knowing that Pyotr is all right and that God would keep the Kachenkos from any more trouble. We have prayed so much! Of course God will answer our prayers."

Poppa gave Momma the kind of look Ivan loved. Something seemed to lift inside Ivan. Playfully, he pulled Katya's pink ribbon.

"What kind of puppet show are you having, Katushka?"

"A group of children are coming from one of the State orphanages. It's such a big orphanage they have their very own school performances all over Moscow."

Momma put Katya's brush away and sat down at the table. Poppa bowed his head for the breakfast prayer. Ivan was always the last to close his eyes. He loved looking at Poppa praying.

As soon as the prayer was over, Katya continued talking as if there had been no interruption. "I don't think I've ever seen real orphans before."

Momma shook her head. "Many of them aren't real orphans, Katya." Suddenly Momma stopped and gave Poppa a regretful look as if she were sorry to have spoken.

Poppa shrugged. "What Momma means, children, is that some of the children are boys and girls who aren't with their parents for one reason or another. Sometimes their parents are temporarily assigned important work far away."

"Or sometimes a parent is in a labor camp!" Ivan said grimly.

Katya looked anxious. "Would Pyotr be in an orphanage, Momma?"

Momma passed Katya some dark bread. "We don't call them orphanages, Katya. He'd be in a boarding school somewhere. A live-in school."

Katya's dark eyes were enormous with thought. Then they brightened. "Wouldn't it be funny if Pyotr came back as one of the puppeteers? He's good with puppets!"

Ivan choked on his glass of yogurt. "Poppa, do you think Pyotr would be in such a school in Moscow?"

Poppa was thoughtful. "Probably not far away, Ivan. Mrs. Kachenko's trial has to be in Moscow if she has one, and at some point in the trial, Pyotr will have to be present for the sentencing."

Katya sighed heavily. "I was going to be happy today, but now the puppeteers will only remind me of Pyotr!" Tears swam in her eyes.

Poppa shrugged into the jacket he wore every day to his factory. "And what about what you told us, young lady? Didn't you have the assurance from the Lord this morning that Pyotr is all right and his family, too?" Poppa waited. "Well, didn't you?"

Katya nodded. A soft smile dimpled her cheek. "Yes, Poppa." Once again her eyes sparkled. "Today will be a happy day!" She jumped up from the table to give Poppa a good-bye kiss. Momma too kissed Poppa. "Don't work too hard, Sergei."

"See you at dinner!" Poppa waved as he closed the door.

It might be a happy day for Katya, Ivan thought glumly as he swept the schoolyard. He had forgotten his gloves and in spite of the pale sunshine his hands were cold. Everyone in school had to labor a certain number of hours a week, from the youngest pupils to the oldest. Usually Ivan liked outdoor work but today he still felt discouraged at what he had done at the KGB office. Poppa had forgiven him, and so had the pastors. And so had God! But the furious words of the officer stuck in his mind. And the strange sudden way he had stopped as if he had said too much. But what had he said? Only that there were dangers to Soviet life within and without. Without. That would mean the outside world. Those who would slander. That was a familiar word. His teachers often mentioned the anti-Soviet "slander" of the foreign radio stations and newspapers. As far as Ivan could tell, they were only telling the truth.

If foreigners knew of Mr. Kachenko's trial, that would give them plenty to say about Soviet life! What if it were possible that there had been a foreigner at the trial? Sometimes foreign newsmen got into the trials.

Ivan's attention was diverted from his thoughts by a boy who was hanging around the gate outside the school. He was old enough to have a job and Ivan wondered why he had nothing better to do than walk around the school looking through the fence or leaning against the front gate. Ivan was surprised that someone didn't come out and tell him to go away or go to work.

Once or twice Ivan thought he detected an inviting look on the boy's face as if he were calling Ivan over to him. Ivan kept sweeping, ignoring the stranger as best he could. Then a terrible thought struck him. What if the young man had been sent to lure him away from school? What if he were a decoy to get Ivan out of the schoolyard and into a waiting car? What if Ivan were supposed to disappear like Pyotr? The police officer's fury haunted Ivan.

His mouth seemed to turn to sand. Quickly he finished the yard near the gate and moved closer to the school, sending up a cloud of dust in the vigor of his sweeping.

At last he finished and hurried indoors to his next class.

Making his way to his seat in the room, Ivan glanced casually out of the window. Leaning against the wall, just inside the gate, the boy waited patiently.

◆Flight

All that day at school Ivan had searched the crowded halls between classes and the schoolyard at lunchtime, hoping against hope to see Pyotr's blond head and wide grin emerge from a group of students. Now with school over for the day, Ivan wondered if he should go by the Kachenko apartment to see if the secret agents were still confining Mrs. Kachenko and Sonya.

But the strange boy in the street frightened Ivan. Ivan tried to see the front gate in the crowds of students that were pouring out of school on their way home. Finally there was a break in the clusters of students. Sure enough, the boy was waiting by the gate and when he saw Ivan he gave a start of recognition. Unmistakably, he was beckoning to Ivan.

Quickly Ivan turned and walked rapidly

back toward the school. There was a small gate on the other side of the building that opened onto an alley. Students were not supposed to use it for an exit but Ivan opened it many times for delivery men with school supplies.

"Ivan! Where are you going?" Katya's voice cut through Ivan like a knife. "Wait for me!" Ivan wondered if he should just run. Then he realized that Katya too might be in danger.

He waved urgently. Mystified, Katya made her way against the flow of the crowds toward him.

"Katya, don't talk. Just do as I say," Ivan commanded.

Frightened, Katya nodded silently and began hurrying beside Ivan. When they reached the back of the school and the small gate, Ivan unbolted it and pushed Katya ahead of him into the alley. Quickly he followed her, bolting the gate behind him. Grabbing her hand, Ivan began to run. Katya was gasping for breath. "Ivan, stop. What's the matter?"

Ivan kept running, determined to reach the safety of the crowded street. When they emerged from the alley they would be a full two blocks from school.

"Ivan, I want to talk to you. I can't run anymore!"

Ivan shook his head insistently. "Katya, we've got to keep going. It's just a little farther."

When they reached the end of the alley they burst into the street, to the astonishment of passersby. Katya leaned against an elm tree in the parkway and tried to get her breath. Her face was crimson with exertion and one of her pink bows was untied and hung limply from her glossy braid.

Ivan wanted to keep walking but knew Katya would not budge until she had both an explanation and a rest.

"You're not supposed to use that gate!" she panted. "We could have gotten into trouble."

Ivan leaned against the tree also. He hoped they looked as if they were waiting for someone. "Katya, all day there has been a strange boy watching me from the street outside school. At first I wasn't sure, but now I know. Perhaps he's been sent to get me—to get us—the way they got Pyotr."

Katya's face was frozen in unbelief.

"I couldn't explain all that when I saw you, Katya..." Ivan's voice trailed off at the expression on Katya's face. Her eyes were as wide as saucers. She was biting her lips to suppress laughter. Ivan stared at her in exasperation. Suddenly Katya began to laugh. She laughed so infectiously that passersby smiled at her in amusement.

Ivan's face reddened. "Katya, stop it!" he hissed. "What's the matter with you? Why are you laughing?"

Katya finally wiped her eyes. "Oh, Ivan," she gasped. "You frightened me so much with all that running. And to think of it!"

"To think of what?" Ivan started walking. He was feeling very foolish, and cross at Katya.

Catching up to him, Katya put her hand on his arm to slow him down. "Ivan, look. I want to show you something."

Ivan glanced irritably at Katya. Out of her pocket she had drawn a small metal object. Quickly she placed it in Ivan's hand and continued walking. Ivan looked at it. It was a boy's penknife. Then a wave of amazement engulfed him. It was Pyotr's penknife! Many times Ivan had admired it and had seen Pyotr use it on walks they had taken together in the woods outside of Moscow.

"Pyotr's pocketknife!"

Katya nodded. "That boy we ran away from. He was waiting all day to find you and give it to you. Somebody pointed you out to him when you were just finishing sweeping. After school I was at the gate and he asked me if I had seen a boy called Ivan Nazaroff. He asked me because he saw I was not wearing the red scarf and he thought we might be acquainted."

Katya giggled. "I told him you were a very strange boy and I tried to stay away from you as much as possible."

"Katya!" Ivan grinned and gave Katya an affectionate push. "What did you really say?"

"I said you were my brother." A puzzled frown crossed Katya's face. "Before I could say another word, he put the penknife in my pocket and vanished into the crowd."

Ivan nodded knowingly. "Of course! Pyotr sent him. He has a message for me from Pyotr."

The children looked at each other in speechless excitement. Ivan grinned suddenly and rubbed his hands together in elation. "Good old Pyotr! I should have known he'd figure out a way to get word to us. It would have been too dangerous to try to reach his mother. But he must be in Moscow and he's sent a messenger!"

The smile faded from Katya's face. She gripped Ivan's arm anxiously. "But the boy we ran away from, what if we don't find him again?"

◆Message from Pyotr

It had been a wretched evening and night.
Momma said Ivan would wear a path in
the carpet, pacing from his desk to the
window all evening, in hopes of seeing the
strange boy on the street. Poppa and Ivan
had gone for a stroll around the block once
after supper and once before bed, but
there was no trace of the stranger. Even
Momma and Katya had invented an excuse
for going to the corner shop after the
dishes were done.

Ivan hadn't been able to concentrate on
his lessons and he knew his homework
had been carelessly done. His teacher
would be sure to notice and reprimand
him in front of the class.

Lying awake in his bed, Ivan's thoughts
were in a turmoil. He tried to imagine
what he would say to his history teacher,
Mara Nicholaevna, about his homework.

He tried to remember what the strange boy looked like. When he dozed, he dreamed of running, running, through alleyways, over balconies, away from agents with dark coats that flapped as they ran, like the dark wings of great birds.

But when morning came he was wide awake and the first one up and dressed. Momma found him standing at the window, staring intently at the street.

She stood quietly behind him and put her arms around his waist. "Ivan, Ivan, the boy will find you again today. Do not worry so much."

Ivan nodded without turning around.

"But even with the penknife, my son, you must be very, very careful. You will promise me?"

"I promise, Momma." Ivan gave her a smile over his shoulder and returned his gaze to the street.

"You will not go with him anywhere. Not for a walk. Not into a car, Ivan."

"No, Momma. And I will keep Katya away. I will remember everything you and Poppa told me last night. And God will be with me."

Momma squeezed Ivan's waist and went into the kitchen to put on the kettle.

Ivan did not see her anxious face or her eyes close in fervent prayer. When she reappeared, she gave Ivan a playful slap.

"Since you are ready so early, you can set the table for breakfast." She put four plates and knives and spoons into his hands.

Ivan made a face. "Women's work!" he joked.

Momma wagged a finger at him. "Not in Soviet Russia, good son! Have you forgotten we have equality of labor?"

Ivan pretended to be grumpy. "Perhaps it was better in the old days," he teased. "Men worked in the fields and women worked in the house. Perhaps it was better then!"

Katya stuck her head into the room with such a shocked look on her face that Momma and Ivan laughed.

Katya yawned and rubbed her face. "I didn't know you were joking."

Ivan frowned at Katya. "Hurry up and get dressed. I want to be early to school today and if you aren't ready, I'll go without you!"

The morning was cold again and the sun was not shining. Katya shivered as she and Ivan walked around the school block a second time.

"He's not here, Ivan," Katya said plaintively. "Please, can't we go inside and get warm? It's silly to keep walking around, and besides it must look very suspicious."

Reluctantly, Ivan agreed. It would look funny for them to walk around the block a third time, and especially on such a raw morning. Walking as slowly as possible, they turned in at the school gate. Katya hurried to her door, glad to get inside the shelter of the building. Ivan made his way more slowly to his entrance on the other side of the school. As he turned the corner of the building, he heard a loud hiss.

"Pssssst! Over here!"

Ivan wheeled in the direction of the sound. His heart pounded in delight. Leaning against the side of the building in a corner of an outside stairway was the strange boy.

"I thought you two would never stop walking around this school!" he began.

Ivan laughed. "We were looking for you."

"I know that. Now listen, I have to talk fast and then I've got to get out of here. I've run away from the school where your friend Pyotr Kachenko is. He knew I was going and asked me to tell you where he is. Rotten thing they did to him, grabbing him off the street like that!"

"Where is he?" Ivan was terrified that someone would come and the boy would run away.

"He's at School 74 on Victory Street. He's all right and he wants his mother to know he's all right and not to worry. You have to take the Metro going west and get off at Victor Square. It's a very long way."

"Can I see him? Can people go there and visit?"

The boy grinned. "Depends on how smart you are. It's not allowed. But neither is running away!"

That morning at home Ivan had been too excited to eat his breakfast. Momma had made him take some bread and hard cheese in his pocket to eat on the way to school. Quickly Ivan pulled it out of his coat. "Thank you with all my heart!" He held the food out to the boy and was startled at how quickly the boy grabbed it.

Ivan felt for his bus fare home. "Here, it's all I have right now. I can walk home." The boy was stuffing the bread into his mouth, but he nodded gratefully and took the few *kopecks* with his free hand.

"Where are you going?" Ivan whispered. The boy shook his head. Ivan nodded. Of course! It would be foolish for the boy to tell. If Ivan were questioned....

Ivan saw that the boy was checking the yard in preparation for leaving. "Thank you again." Ivan held out his hand and the boy, after a moment's surprise, shook it awkwardly. "God go with you," Ivan whispered. The boy nodded vigorously and then walked boldly across the yard. The caretaker, turning in at the gate as the boy left, gave him a mildly curious glance and then shrugged. Ivan leaned against the building in relief.

School 74 on Victory Street... The address burned itself into his memory. Ivan longed to rush out of the schoolyard, to Pyotr's mother, to his father at the factory, to School 74. His mind was churning with emotions and impulses.

"In quietness and confidence shall be your strength." The old verse his mother quoted returned to his memory. Ivan took a deep breath and walked calmly into the school. Before he could do anything he must have a plan.

◆Inside the gate

School number 74 was a large, buff-colored, factory-like building sprawling behind a high stone wall. It had taken Ivan an hour's ride on the Metro to reach Victor Square and another half hour walking to find the school. Ivan wished Katya was with him. He also wished he had a plan. What good was it going to do to walk around the building? But as hard and as long as Ivan had thought, he couldn't figure out how he could get inside the building to see Pyotr.

The front gate was ornate iron. Ivan peered through the decorative grating, strangely out of place for the somber building. Inscribed above the double doors of the school was the slogan, "Master Marxist-Lenin Teaching!" Ivan read the words and quickly looked away.

Some young boys were kicking a ball in

the corner of a playing field. Once in a while
one of them would run into the center of
the yard to retrieve a ball. They were
younger than Katya and were arguing a
great deal. Ivan was surprised. It was
unusual for children to quarrel.

He supposed they didn't have a coach
to help them. They seemed to be trying
to play soccer but couldn't agree on the
rules of the game.

There was a movement at one of the
windows and Ivan turned quickly away
from the gate and began walking.

It was an old part of Moscow, with
narrow side streets opening into wide,
walled courtyards. Many of the large homes
had been made into apartments and Ivan
enjoyed the bits of life that seemed to
spill out of the open windows. A woman
leaned suddenly out of an upper casement
and shook out a tablecloth. She smiled at
Ivan. On a window sill, a collection of lush
plants drank in the pale spring sunshine.
An old man sat by an open window
smoking a pipe.

For a few minutes Ivan forgot about Pyotr
and the school. But as he turned a corner
it loomed ominously again before his
view.

There had to be a way to get in! Ivan leaned against a corner of the wall and closed his eyes. "Lord, you have led me this far. You have brought me safely to this school, but now that I am here I don't know what to do. I know you want me to help Pyotr, but how, Lord? How can I even get inside?"

Ivan's prayer was interrupted by the renewed quarrelling of the boys playing soccer. Their little voices were tight with frustration and anger.

"Your side can't have the ball if you kick it on the pavement. That's out of bounds..." "It's a penalty if you pick the ball up!" "You can pick it up if you are a goalie!" "You can't!" "And besides, you hit the ball with your shoulder, that's not allowed!" "It is so allowed!" "I didn't try to hit it! The ball hit me! That's different!"

Ivan shook his head at the jumble of misinformation. He wished he could shout instructions over the wall to them. Ivan thought of his own soccer coach and how insistent he was that every rule be exactly observed. But he was the best coach Ivan had ever had and Ivan had learned the game in a new way this year.

"It's not enough to be the best

forward, Nazaroff!" the coach was fond of saying. "You've got to know *every* position, *every* play, *every* rule if you want to really master the game!"

Ivan worked hard for Comrade Sinyavsky.

Suddenly a thought struck Ivan. Rapidly he walked toward the heavy iron gate and pushed it open. As he crossed the courtyard to the front door, the boys in the playground stopped their argument to stare. Boldly Ivan raised the heavy knocker on the door and let it fall with a loud thud. Almost immediately the door was opened by a bent old *babushka* who was polishing the inside brass doorknob.

"Please, Grandmother, I wish to speak to the director of this school."

The old woman nodded and without a word led Ivan to a door at the end of the hall. She jerked a bony thumb toward the door and returned to her work.

Ivan looked back at the wide stairway they had passed. His heart was pounding wildly. Somewhere in this building, in one of the rooms, perhaps studying or sleeping or praying was Pyotr. What if he should suddenly appear, walking along the hall or opening a closed door? Or was he locked up somewhere, discouraged, longing for home?

Ivan knocked gently on the heavy oak door of the director's office.

The director was a man with a smooth pale face and almond-shaped eyes. He had a bushy black moustache which he pressed with two or three fingers as he listened.

Ivan hoped his voice didn't sound as shaky as he felt.

"Comrade Director, I am a student at Moscow School number 10. One of my great loves is history—Russian history and also the history of our great capital city, Moscow..." The director showed no reaction to Ivan. He continued sitting in his chair, smoothing his moustache.

"It gives me pleasure to explore the city. This afternoon I have been walking about enjoying this very old section of Moscow."

Ivan paused hopefully. Still the director made no comment. Ivan took a deep breath. "I was walking past your school and I heard some young children trying to play soccer in the playground. Someone told me, Comrade, that this is a live-in school. That the children here are orphans,

mostly. I know that in Socialist life it is our responsibility to help one another to grow up to be strong and good citizens."

The director shifted in his chair. "What is your name?"

"Ivan Nazaroff." Ivan waited politely but the director said no more. Ivan began to feel very uncomfortable.

"I would like to help boys less fortunate than myself. In my school I am a forward on our soccer team. My coach, Comrade Sinyavsky, says I am his best player." Ivan was afraid of seeming to boast. "It is only because our coach is so excellent, Comrade Director."

"What do you want, Nazaroff? I am a busy man." The director folded his arms across his chest and bent forward in his chair. "What are you here for?"

"I would like to volunteer to coach some of the boys here. Perhaps you do not have a soccer coach."

A faint smile crossed the director's face.

"Perhaps I could come a few times and organize a proper soccer team. The boys outside don't seem to know the rules. I should very much like to help them. Perhaps I could just get them started in the right direction."

The director appraised Ivan cooly for a long time. "This is not an ordinary school, Nazaroff. You know that?"

"Yes, Comrade."

"Some of the pupils here are discipline problems, misfits, not all are merely orphans."

"Yes, Comrade."

"Do you think, if you were to help us out for a bit, you could obey my instructions without fail and without question? We have some necessary procedures here."

"Yes, Comrade."

The director hesitated, then seemed to make up his mind. "It might be possible that you could be useful for a day or two." He cleared his throat. "Quite soon there is to be a routine inspection of our facilities. Unfortunately, with our great Soviet educational system expanding as it is, we are short-staffed." Ivan nodded his head in understanding.

"Our physical education program is not what I would like it to be. In fact," the director shrugged slightly, "at the moment, we have nobody." Ivan tried to suppress a feeling of delight that was bubbling up inside him.

"I have intended to spend some time in this area, but other duties have prevented me."

Ivan tried not to look down at the director's desk. Except for an ink blotter, a telephone, a calendar, and a large lamp, it was absolutely clear.

The director stifled a yawn. He pressed his moustache thoughtfully. "Because of the nature of our school I would have to forbid any personal conversations with any of the young boys whatsoever. Can you see to it that they understand this perfectly?"

"Certainly, Comrade. I give you my word I shall refuse any personal conversations with the boys I will be coaching." The director stood up wearily. "The inspection of our educational program is an important event. If it would be possible for you to teach the younger boys some rules of soccer and enough skills so that they could play an exhibition game for the inspectors, that might be most useful to me. Do you think you could manage that in just a session or two?"

"If the boys are willing to work hard, I'm sure I can help them, Comrade."

As he showed Ivan out, the director looked mildly pleased. "You may come in a week."

Ivan stiffened his chest and held his breath against the joy that wanted to break out of him in a grin. At the door, Ivan shook the director's hand formally. "I will do my best, Comrade. It will be a privilege to come here."

A cynical smile crossed the director's face. "I don't want you hanging around. Just a time or two, next week! You shape the boys up and be on your way."

"Yes, Comrade."

On the street, Ivan laughed softly in a wonder of praise. "Thanks, thanks to God!" he repeated.

Now maybe he would be able to make up for losing his temper in the police office.

◆Pyotr must escape!

Momma carefully ladled the steaming red borscht into the wide bowls. All around the crowded table murmurs of appreciation were being raised.

"Nobody makes borscht like my Natasha!" Poppa took a deep sniff as he accepted his bowl.

Mrs. Kachenko, sitting next to Poppa, smiled at the impatience of little Sonya who was banging her spoon on the white tablecloth. "Soup! Sonya! Soup!" she was demanding, her eyes wide with happiness.

Katya patted Sonya's yellow curls in admiration. "You will soon have your soup, Sonychka!" she soothed. "The best in Moscow!" Katya gave a polite glance to Mrs. Kachenko. "...Except for maybe your own Momma's borscht!"

Ivan dropped a huge spoonful of sour cream in his soup and stirred it slowly.

There was so much to discuss. He wished people would stop talking and let Pastor Aranovich pray so the meal could begin. Finally the pastor bowed his head. "We thank you, Father, that you provide for all our needs. We thank you for your Son, Jesus Christ, who gives us new life and freedom in Him." The pastor's voice was steady. "Be with those who are absent from us, especially Brother Kachenko in the labor camp. We praise you that you have counted him worthy to suffer for your sake. Be with Pyotr in the boarding school. Help him to know you are with him, and that he is ever in our prayers. Bless this meal, our Father, and guide our thoughts. In the name of Jesus we pray, Amen."

Momma raised her spoon to her lips with a nod to the children. Katya began feeding the hearty soup to little Sonya. Ivan ate hungrily, breaking off a chunk of dark bread from the loaf in the center of the table and dipping it in some honey.

Poppa cleared his throat. "We agreed that we would meet to discuss what ought to be done about Pyotr. We have prayed much. Now we must plan a little for next week."

Mrs. Kachenko wiped her eyes with a handkerchief. "The Secret Police will never admit that they have taken Pyotr. They insist he must have run away. What can we do?"

Momma looked thoughtful. "They have taken him away to force you to denounce your husband."

Mrs. Kachenko nodded miserably. "They tell me that if I will say what they want, perhaps Pyotr will come home. And I need not fear about charges that I am an unfit mother."

Pastor Aranovich's face was knotted in perplexity. "I do not understand why the police are so determined to have you say such things. What difference does it make?"

The memory of the interview at the police station with Comrade Jarmansky made Ivan feel very uncomfortable. The fury of the officer had so shocked him that even now he could see his face and hear his every word. Ivan wanted to stop his ears at the memory. "There are those who do not understand! Enemies both within and without! Slander! Slander!"

Sometimes Christians got information about their problems to the outside world. If it were printed in foreign papers, it was called slander by the Soviet press. Slander. That's where Ivan had heard the word before.

Ivan wished the story of how Pyotr was taken away from his family could get to the outside world! Ivan almost smiled to himself at the thought of how angry Jarmansky would be then!

"Poppa!" The thought was so sudden that Ivan interrupted something Pastor Aranovich was saying. Poppa frowned at Ivan's impulsiveness. "I'm sorry, Pastor. I just thought of something."

Pastor Aranovich took a spoonful of hot soup with a nod to Ivan. Ivan kept his voice low. "Poppa! Why don't we try to get the story to Christians outside of Russia of how Pyotr was taken away? It was wrong of our government! Why don't we tell it? Perhaps people in the West would protest!"

Ivan thought immediately of the terrified court secretary at the trial. "Even the court secretary thought we ought to protest. Why don't we?"

Pastor Aranovich raised his eyebrows at Poppa. "It is a good thought, Sergei," he said. "Perhaps we could do this."

The words spilled out of Ivan.

"Comrade Jarmansky seemed very worried about news getting out. Remember when he was so angry at me? He talked about slander? And the foreign press? I don't think he meant to say so much, but he did!" Pastor Aranovich nodded. "Perhaps we could do this."

Ivan knew he was the very man to set in motion the many links in the secret chain of communication that believers had with the outside world. Within a few days the story would safely reach the West, if Pastor Aranovich decided.

Mrs. Kachenko broke into the conversation. "But what about Pyotr now? What is to be done about him? How can we get him home?"

Poppa rubbed his chin. "You know, there is something very good in the fact that the police maintain that Pyotr has run away—that they have not removed him."

"How can that be good, Poppa?" Ivan stared at his father in bewilderment.

"If we were to get Pyotr out of that school—if he were to return home—the police would have to pretend to be glad he had returned."

"Of course!" Mrs. Kachenko's eyes were shining. "Tomorrow the police come

again. If I am charged and brought
to trial, I will need Pyotr to defend me.
He will be able to say I am a good mother.
That I do not break the law as the police
will say."

Pastor Aranovich looked at Poppa. "It
is a good thing, Sergei. And Pyotr must
be kept in hiding until we know about the
trial. It would not do when he returns to
have him taken away again."

Katya jumped up from the table and
ran to Ivan with a hug. "It's perfect, Ivan.
All you have to do is get Pyotr out of that
school."

Ivan stared in alarm at the ring of faces
that gazed hopefully at him. "Poppa, how
can I get Pyotr out? I don't know where
he is. It is a very big place. Maybe he is
locked up!"

Momma put another ladle of soup into
Ivan's bowl. "To expect that of Ivan is too
much! It is one thing for him to try to get
a message to Pyotr. An escape is quite
another thing."

Ivan agreed. An escape was quite another
thing!

Poppa gave Ivan a sympathetic nod.
"This is something we are not asking you to
do. Do not feel pressured, Ivan. The Lord

will show us the way to help Pyotr."

Ivan was thinking. Slowly his voice found the words. "The Lord sent the strange boy to me. The Lord helped me to get inside the school. Maybe the Lord will show me how to get Pyotr out."

A quietness seemed to fall upon the room. "Maybe he will," Poppa said gently. "We will pray."

◆The hidden passage

It was a rag-tag group of little boys that Ivan faced in the yard of Moscow school number 74. While the director explained to them that Ivan would be coaching them for an exhibition game Ivan counted the serious faces turned toward him. There were 25 boys in the group. That was enough for teams, Ivan thought. In the equipment room he had found three soccer balls, enough for workouts, and two ragged nets that could be set up for the goalies at the ends of the playing field.

As discreetly as possible, Ivan's eyes roamed to the windows of the school as the director gave the boys his instructions: "No personal conversations with Comrade Nazaroff." "Closest attention to be paid to his coaching." He lectured them on the importance of self-discipline and cooperation. Once Ivan caught a glimpse of a curious face looking out of the windows above him. Ivan tried not to stare or to appear interested in anything except the boys now circled around him, as the director left.

Nervously Ivan cleared his throat. "First of all you have to know how to kick the ball correctly." The boys were listening intently. There was something touching about the way they seemed anxious to please him. Ivan smiled suddenly. "You know, soccer is a lot of fun. I don't want you to be worried about making mistakes. You'll find out that soccer is easy and it's more fun when you really learn it."

A few of the boys smiled shyly at Ivan. It was hard to believe this was the same group that had been shouting and arguing only a few days ago.

"There are three kinds of kicks," Ivan began. "The most common is the kick with the inside of your foot. If you write with your right hand, you'll kick with your right foot. If you're left-handed, then use your left foot. Here's how you do it."

Ivan placed the checkered ball in front of him and kicked the ball a few times down the field and then returned to the group.

"Another kick is with the outside of your foot, like this." Again the boys carefully watched Ivan's demonstration. "The third kind of kick is called a 'toe kick' and that's used when you want to kick the ball fast and far. You don't have control over the ball when you kick like this, but it's a good way of clearing it down the field."

It wasn't long before Ivan had the boys in three lines practicing kicking the ball down the field. They worked hard and were soon flushed and out of breath.

"You need to run around the playing field every day. As many times as you can. Even when I'm not here," Ivan advised. "Could you do this?"

One of the boys, a rather pudgy youngster of about ten, was panting heavily. "Is it true you are a very important soccer player, Comrade Nazaroff? Is it true you have won many games?"

Ivan laughed. "It's never any one player who is important. It is the whole team working together. Everyone on the team is important. It is true that in my school, our team has won many games. But you too can be good. You'll have to learn to run well, though."

The director, watching from the side of

his office window, was pleased at the lines of boys running steadily around the field. Nazaroff had come along at the right time. Hopefully the inspector would be impressed. That was good. And the boys were running off a lot of energy. That too was good. There were enough irregularities at the school as it was. It would be a fine thing to be able to show the inspector that athletics were not neglected.

It was already dusk when the bell rang for the end of the outdoor period. The boys regretfully ended their practice and formed lines to go inside the school. Ivan wiped his face on a towel that hung in the untidy equipment room and looked around. It was his responsibility that the few balls and nets were carefully accounted for. He was anxious that the room be left in perfect order.

It appeared that the room had once been a large kitchen pantry. Apparently the kitchen itself was still in use and Ivan could smell cabbage cooking behind a locked door that once must have opened to the kitchen. Low voices of the cooks rose and fell as Ivan folded the nets and left them on the shelves. It was a poor place, he was thinking. A few balls, some worn jump ropes, some exercise mats. Even the mats were not hung from their straps on the wall hooks, but just tossed in piles on the floor.

Ivan lifted a mat and carried it to a hook. It looked better hanging as it should. Perhaps there were enough hooks to hang all the mats and if the room were swept, it would be greatly improved.

Some of the hooks were loose and needed twisting into the wall before they could support the weight of a mat. The paneling on the walls of the room was expensive and decorative. Ivan thought it was too bad to deface the lovely oak with heavy iron hooks. Some old holes gaped where other equipment had once hung.

A broom stood in the corner of the room and Ivan began sweeping the dusty floor. Dried mud clung to the broom and he shook the dirt off and out of the door, and turned back to sweeping.

"You are a worker!" The voice of the school director startled Ivan. He looked quickly at the door where the director stood. "The room looks better."

"Thank you, Comrade. I thought I

could hang up the mats."

"We don't have much equipment here, Nazaroff, as you can see. Nothing must be missing." Something in his voice made Ivan blush.

"Nothing will be missing, Comrade. I enjoy taking care of equipment."

The director moved away from the door. "Just get the boys going on their soccer playing. That's what I'm looking for." Without a farewell, he was gone.

Ivan leaned heavily against the wall in an alcove corner of the room. What was the use of teaching a few boys soccer and cleaning up a room? He was no closer to finding Pyotr than when he was standing in the street. A hook dangled from the wall beside his head. With a discouraged shrug, Ivan yanked idly at it. It held fast. In surprise, Ivan pulled harder. It had been screwed into the wall at a careless angle and although loose, wouldn't pull free. It didn't matter. It wasn't his job to repair the whole room! Ivan pulled on his jacket in the fading light, and zipped it up. The hook dangled invitingly. With a last effort Ivan gave it a mighty yank. To his complete astonishment the wall itself swung forward, revealing a secret door.

◆Nikolai

For several minutes Ivan stared in amazement at the passageway. As his eyes became accustomed to the dimmer light of the alcove he could see fancy scrollwork decorating the paneling. Cautiously he ran his hand along the inner edge of the door. His fingers stopped as they touched metal. Delicate hinges, covered over with dust, were artfully worked into the fretwork. Ivan peered at the top of the doorframe. He supposed the door opened by a spring of some kind rather than a knob. By yanking the hook he had pressured the spring device and opened the door.

But why a door in an old pantry? A flight of narrow stairs led up into the house. Perhaps it had been a servant's door of some sort so that live-in maids and cooks from the old days could make their way to their rooms at the top of the house.

A bell clanged from somewhere in the building. In the kitchen, Ivan could hear the cooks hurrying to serve supper. Overhead, Ivan heard the thudding of hurrying steps. His own pounding heart seemed to match the footsteps. Perhaps while everyone was eating, he could get inside the building to explore!

As softly as a cat, Ivan crept up the dusty stairs. Every few steps he stopped and listened intently. He was somehow close to the dining room and could hear someone giving instructions about the portioning of the food.

Gradually the voice grew fainter and Ivan found himself on a small landing by a door. Slowly he turned the knob and opened the door a crack. In one direction he could see a long empty hallway. Opening the door farther he looked the other way. The hall ended almost immediately with a small window in the end wall. Doors of classrooms stood open up and down the corridor.

The bedrooms must be on the next floor, Ivan was thinking rapidly. If Pyotr were not eating with the other boys he might be confined to a bedroom. If only he could

actually find Pyotr! Ivan let the door click shut and raced up the next long flight of stairs. Again the stairs stopped before a door at a landing. He pushed it open and peered out.

This time the doors along the hallway were closer together, signifying smaller rooms. Ivan stepped into the corridor and listened. There seemed to be no sound or movement in the room closest to the passageway. Ivan turned the knob silently and pulled open the door, revealing a small, very plain bedroom with several beds. As Ivan quickly closed the door he noticed an odd thing: there was a bolt lock on the outside of the door. Glancing down the hall, Ivan saw that each door was equipped with such a lock. With a sinking feeling he realized the meaning of the bolts: by this means, boys could be locked in their rooms!

"But if Pyotr is locked up, then he would be in a room with the bolt drawn across the door!" Ivan pressed his lips together· in a terrible excitement. If he could find such a lock, perhaps Pyotr would be behind·it.

Ivan moved silently along the corridor, looking eagerly at each door. All the bolts were open. Discouraged, he returned to the passageway door, then noticed a last door between the secret passageway and the end of the hall. His heart gave a lurch! The bolt was drawn! For some reason, this room was locked from the outside. That could only mean someone was inside!

Ivan's hand was shaking so much he could hardly pull back the bolt. It made a harsh scraping noise. Fear stung his mouth. His hand seemed to freeze on the knob. With a tremendous effort he pulled open the door. The astonished black eyes of an angry boy met his. Ivan was too horrified to speak.

"Shut the door, stupid!" the boy hissed.

Ivan instantly closed the door. The two boys faced each other. "Who are you? What are you doing here?" The boy's voice remained low and suspicious.

"I ... I'm looking for a friend." Ivan knew his voice was shaking from the shock. The boy grinned in relief and sat down on a bed.

"How'd you get in here?" There was a look of admiration on his face. "You'll be in for it if you get caught, you know."

Ivan nodded miserably. "I came up

those little stairs next door." The boy
shook his head and rolled his eyes.

"It wasn't hard," Ivan explained.
"There's a sort of secret door in the
equipment room that leads up here..."
Ivan's voice trailed off in dismay.
Perhaps he shouldn't be telling this boy
how to escape.

The boy laughed. "Who are you looking
for?"

"Pyotr Kachenko. He's only been
here a few days."

The boy nodded and shrugged. "He's
eating. You can't see him." The boy looked
Ivan over. "And you'd better not stay
around here very long. They'll be
finished eating soon and then this place will
be crawling with people. You'll get caught
for sure."

"Could I get a message to Pyotr? Is
there any way?"

"What have you got?"

Ivan frowned in perplexity. "I don't
know what you mean."

"If I give him a message for you, what'll
you give me?"

Ivan blushed. "I ... I don't know. I don't
have anything."

"No candy? No money?"

"No. Only my *kopecks* to get home on the Metro. I can't give you those. It takes me an hour by Metro to get home."

The boy finally sighed. "What's the message?"

"Tell him Ivan Nazaroff was here. That I want to talk to him."

"That's not a message, stupid. If you want to talk to him, you've got to plan now."

Ivan felt very stupid. "Of course. But how can it be arranged?" The boy thought a minute. "My name's Nikolai." Ivan nodded. He was beginning to like this strange boy.

"Can you come back at night?" Ivan nodded. "Tomorrow night, then. Ten o'clock. Can you fix the outside door of the equipment room so it won't lock shut?"

Ivan felt a stab of reluctance. "I'll be here tomorrow after school. I guess I could." Nikolai laughed again. Ivan could see Nikolai was enjoying himself. "You won't get in if you don't! Come up here to the third floor again and Pyotr will meet you on the landing. I'll have him waiting for you."

"Ten o'clock?"

"Yes. If Pyotr's not here when you come, wait for him. Sometimes there are room checks at night."

Ivan nodded anxiously. He felt he ought to be leaving.

Nickolai stood up and opened the door cautiously and glanced down the hall. "They're still eating."

"Good." Ivan took a deep breath. "I'll go now." He paused in embarrassment. "I suppose I'll have to lock you in again." Nikolai grinned, "Oh yes, you'll have to lock me in. That's not the problem."

Something in Nikolai's face bothered Ivan.

"What's the problem?"

"How are you going to get back out? Those passageway doors lock automatically from the other side. They can't be opened from our corridor."

◆Poppa's urgent advice

Ivan stared in terror at the amusement on Nikolai's face. "The passage doors lock from the other side?"

"Well, of course! You don't think they would leave them open for us to use, do you?"

Nikolai lifted up his mattress and felt inside the coils of a bedspring. In a moment he had a thin, curved bit of metal in his hand.

"Oh, come on, Ivan! You are brave enough to get in here. Don't look so sick!"

The two boys crept into the hall. Deftly, Nikolai shoved the homemade key into the old lock. In a moment there was a click and he pulled the door open.

"Put your shoe in it. Hurry up!"

For a second, Ivan hesitated and then

understood. His shoe would hold the
door open while he locked Nikolai back in
his room. Nikolai chuckled. "We have
secret meetings in the passageway any
time we want. We've been to the bottom.
We even know about the door down
there. But it's never opened for us. I think
the spring's gone funny for our side."

Before he closed Nikolai's door, Ivan
held out his hand. "Thank you, Nikolai.
Until tomorrow."

Nikolai nodded and shook Ivan's hand
vigorously. "You're a good soccer player,
Ivan," he said with a mischievous
twinkle.

Ivan bolted the door with a smile. So it
had been Nikolai Ivan had seen watching at
the window! Quickly picking up his shoe,
Ivan hurried down the narrow stairs to
the bottom.

With tremendous relief he saw the door
still standing open. In an instant he slipped
through it into the equipment room and
closed it behind him. His knees felt
weak. It was now dark outside. In a
moment's time, Ivan was on the street and
walking to the subway. Inside School
number 74, the bell rang for the end of
supper.

Katya's eyes shone with admiration as Ivan told his story. Poppa laughed, trying to make light of the danger, poking Momma in the ribs to make her relax and smile.

"It's not so serious, Natasha—a boy exploring a school." Poppa shook out his handkerchief and blew his nose.

Ivan took a bite of sausage from the supper Momma had saved for him. Katya poured steaming amber tea into his glass. Ivan stretched and popped a lump of sugar into his mouth. Holding the sugar between his teeth he sipped the tea through the sugar the way he had seen his grandfather do it. Momma made a face.

"Ivan's feeling silly, Momma!" Katya laughed in enjoyment. Ivan gave her a tired wink and crunched down on the sugar. He breathed in the steam from the tea and shut his eyes. He felt too tired to think.

"Tomorrow you have another coaching session with the schoolboys?" Ivan opened his eyes. Poppa was looking at him thoughtfully. Ivan could see he was thinking about many things.

"Yes." The thought of school the next day, then the long subway ride, the hours of coaching, and all before he could see Pyotr at ten o'clock made Ivan groan in fatigue.

Poppa handed Ivan a closely written piece of paper. Ivan looked at it curiously. He sat up straight to read it in the light of the lamp.

"It is a translation of the story about Pyotr and his father. Pastor Aranovich managed to get it to a newspaper in the West," Poppa explained.

Ivan gasped in pleasure. "Oh, Poppa, they printed it!"

Poppa nodded. "It is amazing that we in Moscow received news of it so quickly. It was published only a few days ago. A tourist brought it in."

Ivan jumped to the part in the story about Pyotr. He read how Pyotr Kachenko had been illegally taken away from his family by the Secret Police.

"But it has not helped the Kachenkos." Momma began taking the hem down on one of Katya's summer dresses. "We had hoped that perhaps the publicity would make the police afraid to bring Mrs. Kachenko to trial. But it has not."

"Think how angry it will make Comrade Jarmansky!" Ivan grinned shyly at Poppa.

Poppa returned his smile. Then his face became serious. "Ivan, it is important that Pyotr return home. We don't know when his mother's trial will be, but it could come any day. Do you think you can bring Pyotr out with you tomorrow night?"

Ivan swallowed hard.

Katya was ready for bed and stood in the doorway in her white nightgown. Her long brown hair waved around her shoulders. "But if Pyotr escapes, then the newspaper story won't be true! Pyotr will be free. People will think we made up the story."

Ivan looked at Poppa in concern.

Poppa gave Katya a good-night hug. "What you say might be true, Katushka. And nothing would please the Secret Police more! But it is essential that Pyotr be at his mother's trial. If he is able to say she is a good mother and has never broken Soviet laws by taking him to church, then we can hope the court will not take the children away." Poppa kissed Katya. "So you see, Pyotr must come home."

Momma spoke softly. Her voice was anxious. "Do you think you can do it, Ivan? Will it be safe for you?" Tears filled her eyes. "It is a terrible thing for children to be taken away from their mothers."

Ivan shrugged nonchalantly. He spoke with more confidence than he felt. "Tomorrow I can be finished with the coaching. Tomorrow I will help Pyotr escape!"

◆Contact!

Ivan made his way through the afternoon crowds like a sleepwalker. All day in school he had yawned, and now, making his way to the Metro station, Ivan paid no attention to the bustle on the streets. It was the first really warm day in spring. Clustered around the entrance to the Metro station were little stalls or tables covered with white cloths. Behind them, workers in white aprons and caps sold eggs and early flowers.

Even the shoe repair booth was open, with a little man inside rearranging rows of laces and bottles of polish. His eyes sparkled with pleasure and he studied the passing feet of the crowds as if glad at last to see shoes instead of the heavy boots of the bitter winter.

The familiar smell of polish and leather wafted out to Ivan as he passed. Spring was really here! But Ivan was too tired to be elated. All night he had tossed and dozed, too tense about Pyotr to fall into a sound sleep. Now that he was into the day, he could hardly stay awake. Ordinarily, riding the Metro was exciting. But today Ivan passed beside the huge murals and marble walls without admiration. Chandeliers sparkled above his head, but he didn't bother to give them a glance. Thankfully, he sank into his seat on the train as the doors silently closed and the train pulled away.

"Too many late nights!" his teacher Mara Nicholaevna had scolded. "It is your duty to get enough sleep, Ivan Sergeyevich!"

Ivan closed his eyes and the motion of the train made him doze. His head rolled gently with the train. In a little while he would have to summon the energy to coach the boys at School 74. What if the director suspected that Ivan was up to something? It didn't matter. Ivan sighed deeply and shifted in his seat. The image of the narrow passageway came into his mind. He pictured the equipment room, the dangling hook. The hook seemed to be swaying with the movement of the train. In a few moments, Ivan was sound asleep.

He awoke with a start and gazed wildly out of the train, jumping to his feet. It was his stop!

"Thank you, Lord! Thank you for waking me up!" Urgently he pushed toward the door. In a few minutes he was on the street, taking great gulps of the fresh spring air. His nap had refreshed him tremendously.

The boys were waiting for him as he pushed open the iron gate and jogged to the playing field. Ivan was pleased that many of the boys were running around the field. Others were practicing kicks. A few were arguing.

"You're no good. You lose control of the ball all the time." "You kick too far!" "I do not!" "Well, you do! You can't even catch up to the ball after you kick it." "I don't want to! I'm moving it down the field!" "Well, you kick farther than ten feet. Ivan says ten feet is the limit!"

Ivan held up his hand and blew his whistle. The boys drew up into two lines as Ivan had taught them.

"As I promised, today we will have a game first off. You must pick teams and one team will be the sleeves-up team, one the sleeves-down team." Some of the boys began to roll up the sleeves of their white shirts.

A few older boys were strolling around the side of the field. Ivan glanced hopefully at the group, but Pyotr was not among them. Soon Ivan was absorbed in arranging the forwards and full backs and half backs in their places and calling out the centers for the face-off.

Ivan was amazed at how quickly and well the boys played when they wanted to. He knew the director would be pleased. As he watched, questions about the boys filled his mind. Who were they? Which were the orphans? Which were the discipline problems? Were some of them Christians like Pyotr? He felt sad not to be seeing them after today.

"Stay between your man and the goal!" Ivan shouted and blew his whistle. "You've got to keep with the man you're guarding. You've also got to keep your eyes on the ball! Now stay with your man! Stay between him and the goal!"

Ivan's whistle's blast sent the teams racing down the field. The older boys, watching on the edge of the field, began to shout and cheer the teams on. Ivan grinned. That would be good for the players! He looked over at the spectators with a shock of recognition. Cheering the teams with wild enthusiasm was Nikolai!

Ivan froze for a second and then pulled his attention back to the team, his thoughts a sudden jumble. Did Nikolai have a message for him? But something was going wrong with the game! Ivan blew his whistle. The sleeves-up had taken over and were scoring repeatedly.

The sleeves-down had begun to argue and push. Ivan called the teams to a grassy spot in the field for a rest. The boys threw themselves on the ground. Out of the corner of his eye Ivan watched the movement of the small group of older boys. They were strolling slowly back to the building. Ivan stood up just as Nikolai paused at the doorway.

Seeing that Ivan was watching, Nikolai gave a single, deliberate, "yes" nod and a broad wink before turning into the school. Ivan felt a rush of gratitude. It was good of Nikolai to let him know the meeting with Pyotr was set. Ivan wished there was something he could do for Nikolai.

Instead, he called the boys to return to

the game. In moments they were rushing down the field, guarding more carefully, kicking with surprising skill.

"I've come out to thank you, young Comrade." Ivan turned to see the director wrapping his coat more tightly about him in the coolness of the setting sun. The director watched the boys playing. "Just a bit of attention and organization has paid off. They look all right."

Ivan checked his stopwatch at the same moment as the sleeves-down scored a goal. His whistle blast ended the game. The boys clustered around Ivan, anxious to say good-bye with a handshake. The director permitted this show of friend-liness with a certain tense restraint. When the last boy had gone, the director, too, shook Ivan's hand.

"I appreciate your help, Nazaroff. But I do have to ask that you consider this the end of your assignment."

Ivan nodded. "I understand, Comrade."

"I think you do. I explained that your being here at all is a bit irregular. Thank you again, Nazaroff. I'll carry on with the boys where you left off."

Carrying the balls to the equipment room, Ivan wondered. At the door, he bent over and picked up a small twig.

Inside, he saw that everything had been properly put away. The boys had done a neat job with the nets and supporters. Tossing the balls into a corner, Ivan broke the stick. Quickly he thrust the small piece of wood between the door and the frame. Pulling the door closed, he bent anxiously to check the lock. With the door shut, he could just see the smallest tip of the twig preventing the lock from clicking.

Ivan hurried to the subway. There was homework to do before he returned at ten o'clock! As if he could concentrate!

◆Reunion

During soccer practice, Ivan had checked
the best place to come over the school
wall. He had decided on a hilly part of
the playing field where the distance from
the top of the wall to the ground would be
reduced by the rise in the ground. From
there he could make his way to the
equipment room.

Moving rapidly along the shadows of the
rambling old building Ivan prayed
fervently. A wind rattled the trees. "Lord,
let the stick in the lock hold...." What if
the twig had fallen out, or the wind had
blown the door shut, or someone had
entered the equipment room after Ivan
had left, and locked the door? Ivan had no
idea what he would do. There was a patch
of moonlight by the door, but the knob
was hidden in darkness. Ivan could see no
trace of the small pale tip of the thin stick.

With shaking hands he pushed the door. It opened so easily and unexpectedly that he almost fell into the blackness of the room.

Ivan wished he had thought to bring a flashlight. In the total darkness of the room he had to feel his way very slowly along the wall to the small alcove. Not a sound must be made. Nikolai had said there were often room checks at night. People moving about near the kitchen might easily hear noises. Ivan had almost reached the alcove when he heard a movement in the room. His heart lurched in fear. Was someone waiting in a dark corner to catch him? The blood pounded in his ears. The sound was too close to be the night breeze. A faint rustle was repeated. Ivan stared into the blackness, trying to make out an outline or a movement in the deep shadows of the room. His heart raced.

Again the slight rustle returned and then a scurry of tiny claws sped across the wood floor. Ivan leaned weakly against the wall. A mouse! But the experience left him shaking. Suddenly he felt he could not go through with the escape.

It would be better for Pyotr. If they were caught, terrible things might happen to them. Perhaps Nikolai was an informer and had already set up a trap for Ivan and Pyotr. Why had he been so willing to help? The house was suspiciously silent. There were no sounds at all to be heard inside. Surely that was unnatural. It must mean people would be waiting to grab him if he opened the alcove door.

Poppa would understand. Pyotr would go back to bed thinking something had gone wrong. Momma would be glad. Katya's shining eyes reproached Ivan. But what did Katya know about it? She wasn't the one who had to go jumping over walls at night.

Ivan had made up his mind to go home when a strange thing happened. At first he almost felt Poppa was with him, although he knew he was alone in the room. His heart stopped pounding wildly. His thoughts seemed to clear. He could never explain it afterward, but oddly, the room seemed not so dark although he was not aware of a light. His shaking stopped and he felt warm.

A feeling of joy went over him.

"Is it You, Lord?" Ivan barely formed the words. He felt encircled by a "Yes." Softly, smiling in wonder, Ivan reached above his head and pulled hard on the hook. The passageway door swung open with a terrible creak.

Ivan had not noticed the creak before! The noise went through him like a sword. As silently as he had ever moved, he began to creep up the narrow stairs. The blackness seemed to choke him. He felt blind.

He reached the second floor landing and stood still. Not a sound came from above him. He wet his lips and took a deep breath. Step by step he moved upward to the third floor landing. A whisper reached him in the darkness. "Ivan?"

"Pyotr!" Ivan rushed the few remaining stairs and was caught in one of Pyotr's bear hugs.

"Ivan! Oh, Ivan, thank you! Thank you for coming!"

Ivan was softly laughing and hugging Pyotr in the darkness. "Are you all right?"

"Oh, yes. Is Momma all right? And Sonya?"

"Yes! Yes!" Ivan pulled Pyotr down with him to sit on the top stair. "Pyotr, you must listen carefully to me for a moment. Poppa agrees with me that you must leave this place tonight ... with me."

Ivan could feel Pyotr draw back in astonishment. He kept his voice very low. "But, Ivan, if I run away, it will be worse for Momma. And they will only bring me back here again."

"No! The authorities won't admit that they took you. They say you ran away. If you come out with me, you can stay with other Christians until the trial, and then testify."

"What trial?" Pyotr's voice was sharp with fear.

"Pyotr, your mother is going to trial. They say she is an unfit mother. It is really because she will not say bad things about your father. But in the trial they hope to prove that she neglects you and Sonya and takes you to illegal Christian meetings. Sonya is too little to tell the truth. You must come ... to help your mother."

Ivan felt Pyotr stand up in the dark.

"Let's go." His voice was grim but Ivan felt a quick squeeze on his arm. "You lead the way."

◆Trapped

Pyotr had no sooner spoken the words than the boys grabbed one another in terror. There was a repeated, distant clicking sound from the bottom of the narrow passageway. Ivan's heart thudded.

"What is it?" Pyotr tried to laugh off his fear. "It can't be anything."

Ivan listened intently, trying to picture the secret door and the equipment room. A cold draft spun up the stairs to the boys.

Ivan moved forward in relief. "It's the wind, Pyotr. The door at the bottom is swinging in the wind. Hurry! It makes so much noise!"

The boys started down the stairs, feeling their way along with their hands flattened against the passage wall. A spider ran over the back of Ivan's hand. He shuddered and pulled his hand away.

"A spider," he whispered in

explanation to Pyotr. Pyotr was holding onto the back of Ivan's jacket with one hand and the wall with the other.

The clacking of the door became louder as they moved toward it. Suddenly the noise stopped. There was a stillness in the passageway. Ivan paused in a second of uncertainty. They were almost at the bottom. A strong breeze hit his face followed by a final loud click.

"No!" Ivan was so dismayed he forgot to whisper.

"Shhh!" Pyotr's voice was urgent. "Keep going! What's the matter?"

Ivan pulled away from Pyotr and made it to the bottom of the stairs. He pushed hard against the closed door. It was tightly shut. Desperately Ivan put his back against it and shoved.

Nikolai's words returned to him with terrible force: *We know about the door down there. It's never opened for us. I think the spring's gone funny from our side.*

"Ivan, what's the matter? What's wrong with the door?" Pyotr's voice was insistent. "What's wrong?"

Ivan tried to think. He tried to answer Pyotr calmly. "Pyotr, the wind blew the door shut. It doesn't open from this side.

Nikolai told me. We can't get out." Pyotr sat down. "We've got to think." Ivan nodded. Something in the quietness reminded him of the moments in the equipment room when he had felt warmed and happy. "The Lord is with us, Pyotr," he whispered. "I know the Lord will get us out."

Pyotr's voice was discouraged. "You don't know what it's like here, Ivan. Everything's locked. There's no way out."

"Oh, yes, there is!" Ivan insisted. "If the Lord could take the children of Israel out of Egypt, he can take us out of this school!"

Pyotr's voice was low. "But how?"

"Well, since the door is shut, we'll have to go through the school..."

"No!" Pyotr's whisper was explosive. "We can't! Older boys monitor the upstairs until midnight. And I told you, everything is locked!"

Ivan pushed against the door again. It made no movement. "If only I'd left my shoe between it and the wall! I should have thought of the wind!"

Pyotr groaned, "I could go back to bed, but what can we do with you? You've got to get out."

"And if I get out, so do you!" Ivan declared. He hesitated a moment and put his hand on Pyotr's arm. "Pyotr, we're going to have to go through the school. We can't just stay in this passage. We can get onto the second floor if we want, but once we leave the passageway we can't get back in. Is the second floor best?"

Pyotr opened his mouth to protest, but Ivan stood up. "We've got to, Pyotr! Which floor?"

Pyotr began to whisper a prayer. Even though it was dark Ivan shut his eyes. "God in heaven, Ivan and I need your help. Please, Lord ... please ... show us how to get out and keep us safe. In Jesus' name, Amen."

"Amen." Ivan repeated. After a moment he whispered, "Which floor?"

From the way Pyotr answered, Ivan knew that he had made up his mind to try. "There are monitors on the third floor sitting one at each end of the hall. We would be seen right away if we went out on three."

"How did you get into the passageway then?" Ivan asked in admiration. Pyotr laughed softly. "Nikolai got one of his friends to start a fight with one of the monitors. The other monitor went down to try to sort it out and while they were all arguing, he unlocked the door for me."

The boys were creeping up the stairs. "Nikolai is a good sort," Ivan whispered. "Why is he here?"

"His father is a scientist. His mother's dead. The government doesn't like his father so they sent him to work on a dam in Siberia. Nikolai had to stay in Moscow."

"Why don't they like him?"

"Don't know. He criticizes the government."

The boys were on the second floor landing. Ivan felt for the coldness of the doorknob and grasped it. "Are all the rooms on this floor classrooms?"

"And a couple of offices. I don't think anyone will be in them. But where will we go then? We can't walk out the front door! You should see the locks on it!"

Ivan wished he had a better idea of the inside of the school. "What other doors are there?"

Pyotr shook his head in the darkness. "They're all locked, Ivan. With keys. I keep telling you—they lock everything up!"

"What about the basement? Do you

know how to get down there?"

Yes."

"Maybe there's a window we could open, Pyotr. We've got to try something!"

"I know a back way to the basement." For the first time there was a faint note of hope in Pyotr's voice. "We won't have to go down the main staircase."

"Good! Come on, then!" Cautiously, Ivan turned the knob and the boys crept into the dim light of the second floor corridor.

◆An unexpected joy

A white moon, riding low in the late March sky, cast ghostly paths of light across the classroom floors and out into the corridor. Somewhere a loose window pane rattled in the wind. Shadows moved on the walls. The double french doors of the classrooms glittered in the shifting light.

Pyotr was leading the way now, creeping along the sides of the hall, pausing before each classroom door before darting past. A gust of wind made a window shake hideously. Overhead, the boys could hear the thudding of steps.

The corridor seemed to stretch out endlessly before them. Ivan was thinking how like a nightmare it was when suddenly, as Pyotr was crossing in front of a classroom door, an arm shot out and pulled him inside!

Before Ivan could even cry out, he too

was pulled into the dark room. Violently, he yanked himself away from the arm, struggling against someone holding him fiercely by the jacket. Pyotr's voice cut the silence. "Ivan, stop! It's Nikolai!"

With a gasp of relief Ivan slumped against a desk and turned to his captor. "Nikolai! You almost scared me to death." Nikolai grinned and waved the boys to some desks in a dark corner of the room.

Pyotr was laughing and shaking his head. "Nikolai! Don't you ever go to bed?"

"Not when there's excitement afoot!" Nikolai eased into a seat and stretched his long legs out in front of him. Hands in pockets, he gazed at the two boys. "That was bad luck having the door slam shut."

Ivan's mouth dropped open in astonishment. Pyotr stared at Nikolai. "How did you know?"

Nikolai tipped his head back and surveyed Ivan and Pyotr with amusement. "Well, when there's something going on, I want to see it. After I got you out on the third floor landing, Pyotr, I took myself downstairs and out onto the second floor landing to see how you two made out. Thought I might even join you for the fun of it. Not to run away, you understand,

but I go in and out whenever I want. I've never gone through the secret door, though."

Ivan's voice was tight with eagerness. "You know other ways out then, Nikolai?"

"Of course."

Pyotr looked troubled. He kept his voice so low as he leaned toward Nikolai that Ivan had to strain to hear him.

"Nikolai, if you're caught trying to help us escape, it will be very bad for you. You are seventeen."

Nikolai shrugged. "That's not important. You boys interest me. Pyotr, your friend takes such risks for you. He is frightened. He is inexperienced. Yet he becomes very brave. In the passageway you talked about God. You prayed. That's very interesting."

It was Ivan's turn to grin. "You are right about me, Nikolai. I am scared! It is God who gives me courage."

Pyotr cleared his throat. "And you are taking risks for me, Nikolai."

"Because it amuses me. And I am never caught. I am too smart." Nikolai praised himself in a matter-of-fact way that Ivan liked. Nikolai wasn't boasting, he was explaining. "This talk about God ... You both really believe that there is a God?"

"Of course." Ivan kept his voice soft.
"For hundreds and hundreds of years the
Russian people have known God exists
and have prayed to Him and trusted
Him. You know this, Nikolai." Nikolai
nodded. Ivan nodded also. "I love history
and have read a lot of it. No matter what the
history books say, we know that God has
always existed for Russians and for the
whole world."

Pyotr quietly moved his desk slightly
closer to Nikolai. "My father is in a labor
camp for believing in God. If God does
not exist, why would people be arrested
for teaching others about Him? Why
would they have to suffer?"

Pyotr's voice trembled and broke. He
tried to clear his throat. The boys were
silent for a moment. Finally, Nikolai
spoke again.

"If there is a God, He must be angry at
the world. Such terrible things are done."

A feeling of joy swept over Ivan.
Suddenly he knew why the wind had
blown the door shut.

"Nikolai," Ivan's whisper was urgent.
"God loves you. The whole Bible tells of
this love. God came into the world as

Jesus Christ to show love and to die for
the terrible things that men do. He was
punished, not us. This is love, is it not?"

Nikolai grinned. "I have a Bible."

Pyotr sat up in astonishment.
"Nikolai!"

Nikolai laughed softly. "I gave away a
tape recorder to get it. I don't know why.
I read it sometimes, just because it is
forbidden. I don't understand it very
much."

"Jesus died for you." Ivan's voice spoke
quietly in the darkness. "Somehow I think
you know that, Nikolai."

Nikolai suddenly stopped joking. "But
what am I to do? That doesn't bring back
my mother or return my father from
Siberia." His whisper was angry.

"You don't want to give your life to
Communism."

"No. Of course not. I see what it can
do to my father..." he waved a hand at
Pyotr. "To your father...."

"Give your life to God, then! Nikolai! It
is so simple. It is just making up your mind.
Once and for all. It is just giving yourself
to God. Jesus shed His blood for you."

There was silence in the room. Pyotr
and Ivan waited a long time. Finally, in a

very hushed voice Nikolai spoke, "I will do this."

Tears rushed to Ivan's eyes. He could hear Pyotr's gasp of joy beside him. Nikolai was gently laughing, shaking his head and holding it with both hands. "Suddenly I feel so happy! What a strange thing that I feel so happy!"

Ivan gave Nikolai a Russian hug. "It is good that you feel so happy. The feeling may leave you, sometime. But God never will! You will never again be alone!"

Across the room, above a blackboard, a huge picture of Vladimir Lenin caught a gleam of moonlight. Oblivious to Lenin's stern gaze, the three boys bent their heads in prayer.

◆Nikolai eavesdrops

In the end it had been so easy to escape from the tightly locked school that Ivan and Pyotr almost had to pinch themselves some moments later as they hurried safely down the street toward the Metro.

Nikolai had been greatly amused at their astonishment. Swiftly he had led them down a back flight of stairs—not to the basement, where he said all the windows were nailed shut, but to the wide kitchen with its broad serving tables and huge pans that hung glittering in the moonlight.

Mystified, Ivan and Pyotr had watched Nikolai pull a table away from the wall. It had been pushed against an old door.

"To the equipment room!" he had whispered.

Ivan understood. Of course. He had already seen that locked door from the other side. He had watched nervously as Nikolai turned the knob and checked. It held fast against his pull.

With elaborate unconcern Nikolai had pulled his home-made key from his pocket and slid it into the lock. After a moment's effort he had turned the knob and grandly opened the door.

Pyotr and Ivan had hesitated before the open door. Nikolai gave them a shove. "I can get out anytime I want. They would only bring me back. This isn't a bad place. And my father should be coming home soon."

With a pang of sadness, Ivan had seen the door close, and heard Nikolai's little key working the lock shut.

As the Metro sped home through the Moscow night, Ivan and Pyotr were alone in the car. They were silent, each mind whirling with the events of the evening.

Finally, Pyotr spoke aloud a thought that had returned again and again to each of them. "At least he has a Bible, Ivan. It's wonderful he has a Bible to read."

Ivan nodded. The Lord had done wonderful things.

It was hard for Ivan to settle down to school work after the excitement of the past days. And he wished Pyotr could have returned to his mother and to school. But the pastors had decided it would be best for him to hide with a Christian family. No one knew what the authorities might do about his running away.

When Poppa wasn't praying about it, his eyes twinkled in amusement. "Well, the police cannot go to Mrs. Kachenko and complain that her son has run away from their boarding school. They have said all along that they had nothing to do with his disappearance. And if the boy turns up just at the time of his mother's trial, well, what is to be done about that?"

Poppa sat down in his favorite chair and pulled the copy of the foreign newspaper article about the Kachenkos out of a poetry book where he had carefully hidden it. He chuckled and shook his head as he refolded the paper in satisfaction. "I'd like to know what the police think about that!"

What the police thought about it was being discussed at that very moment in Moscow School number 74.

"Surely it is impossible that the boy is

not here!" Comrade Jarmansky's face flushed with fury. "We have had no report of this. Why have we received no report?"

The director pressed his moustache nervously. "Comrade, we do not know how such an escape could have been possible. I have been investigating the matter. Naturally, your office is to receive a full report."

Jarmansky paced the floor in anger. "Do you understand this case has international implications? International implications!"

The director clasped his hands together in an effort to compose himself. "No, Comrade, I had no idea...."

"It is your job to operate this institution efficiently! It is not necessary that you have ideas! There is a story in a foreign paper that one Pyotr Kachenko was removed from his home illegally ... in an effort to force his mother to denounce her prisoner husband. What do you say to that?!"

The director began to shake slightly. He pressed his hands against his desk to steady himself. "Terrible. Terrible lies! Clearly slander against our glorious Soviet state."

Jarmansky coughed irritably. "Not

lies! Not lies, Comrade Director!"

The director took a deep breath. "No," he nodded cautiously. "Not lies."

Comrade Jarmansky threw his heavy form into a chair. "And it is not so simple a matter as merely concerning the boy. A certain trial was also mentioned in this newspaper story. A trial where it was necessary that some irregularities take place. Procedures that foreigners could use to slander our Soviet state. Concerning this trial, there has been a formal protest by some Christian pastors. The news story was part of this 'protest.' Agitators! Troublemakers!" Jarmansky coughed violently in anger.

The director anxiously poured a glass of water from a pitcher on his desk and handed it to Jarmansky. When he had drained the glass, he banged it on the desk and wiped his mouth with the back of his hand.

"There has been an international disturbance about this article in the foreign paper. Letters and protests have been received here in Moscow. It is essential that we prove this story to be false. It has been decided that the boy be returned to his mother." Jarmansky stared, furiously, at the director. His voice became deadly

calm. "How would you suggest I do this?"

The director blinked repeatedly. He pressed his moustache so tightly, his lips stung. He tried to think. "But wouldn't the boy have gone ... uhh ... back? Back to his mother?"

Jarmansky sat motionless staring at the director. His voice remained absolutely quiet. "Naturally, I checked. He is not there."

The director cautiously cleared his throat. His voice was unsteady. "As I reported to you ... Comrade ... we are investigating ... the escape. It is possible ... that we will produce some ... information..."

Jarmansky leaped to his feet so suddenly the director too jumped up in self-defense. Jarmansky leaned across the desk.

"You will produce the boy!" he shouted. "We must have the boy immediately! I have orders to attack the foreign press for slander! A story must appear in *Pravda* proving that the foreign newspaper printed lies! Do you understand?" Furiously, Jarmansky stamped out of the room. As he yanked open the front door he turned toward the director's office. "What sort of place is this?" he roared. The door slammed.

Nikolai, crouched behind the sofa in the director's office, could have told him what sort of place the school was. Instead he shifted himself to a more comfortable position in his tight space to wait until the director left his office. Then, Nikolai thought, he might take a brief absence from the school himself.

◆Ivan strikes a bargain

Even though he was walking slowly, Ivan knew his steps were bringing him closer and closer to the police station and to Comrade Jarmansky. Ivan took long deep breaths and tried to concentrate on his plan.

But he couldn't help smiling, remembering Nikolai's sudden appearance at his bus stop a few days earlier after school. They had hurried to a small park to talk.

Ivan bought some ice cream from the woman who kept the stall in the park and they found a secluded bench.

"But how did you know where to find me?" Ivan could tell from the merriment in Nikolai's eyes how much he had enjoyed surprising Ivan.

"You know the boy who first gave you the message from Pyotr?" Ivan looked blankly at Nikolai.

"You know, the boy with Pyotr's penknife?"

"Oh, yes!" That day seemed so long ago Ivan had almost forgotten it.

"He was a friend of mine. I knew where he was going. Knew you went to Pyotr's school. It was easy."

Everything seemed easy for Nikolai. Even hiding in the director's office.

Nikolai put on a comically grave face. "But Comrade Nazaroff, I knew the meeting would be a significant one. Anytime a boy escapes from our school, there is a meeting in the director's office well worth attending. It is most amusing."

Ivan shook his head helplessly. But even now, on his way to the police station, Ivan was aware of how much he owed Nikolai. If it hadn't been for him, he and Pyotr might not have escaped from the school. If it hadn't been for him, Ivan would not have been able to form this one last plan.

Ivan had listened in amazement at the report given by Nikolai. Suddenly Pyotr was an essential link in the plan of the police to discredit the foreign story! But that link was missing. Perhaps a bargain could be made!

Nikolai had laughed in delight and clapped Ivan on the back. "It is a wonderful plan, Ivan! But you will need great courage."

That was the part Ivan didn't like.

An old woman sweeping the street gave Ivan a curious look as he turned into the police station. Ivan tried to look assured. He knew he was playing a dangerous game. He paused before opening the door to repeat again a verse well-worn in his mind: "My help comes even from the Lord who has made heaven and earth." Inside, his stomach knotted as he asked to see Comrade Jarmansky.

Jarmansky viewed Ivan curiously. "Have I seen you before?"

"Yes, Comrade." Ivan began, interrupted irritably by Jarmansky. "Speak up. I can't hear you if you whisper!"

Ivan took a deep breath and began again. "Yes, Comrade. I was here some time ago with my father, Sergei Nazaroff, and some pastors in connection with the Kachenko case."

Jarmansky eased himself into a large chair and gave Ivan a piercing look.

"Why are you here?"

"I was wondering, Comrade, if you have any further news of Pyotr Kachenko. He was my friend."

Jarmansky closed his eyes for a second, then opened them and looked at his watch. "I am a busy man, young Comrade. I do not have time for visits with schoolboys about their friends. Please." Jarmansky nodded his head sharply toward the door.

Ivan stood his ground. "I have heard that there is a story about my friend in a foreign paper. It says he was taken away by the authorities. That he did not run away from home as you say."

Jarmansky stared at Ivan with astonishment. "What are you saying? That someone gives you anti-Soviet newspapers to read?"

"I am not saying that, Comrade." The two pairs of eyes appraised each other carefully.

Jarmansky shrugged. "It is unfortunate that you have heard such a rumor. Of course you know that the foreign press takes delight in slandering our society."

"It would be a fine thing if Pyotr were at home, would it not, Comrade Jarmansky? Then perhaps a reporter from *Pravda* could take his picture and show that our authorities did not remove him and place him in a boarding school as the foreign story says."

The officer stared at Ivan intently, then abruptly stood up and went to the door. Ivan's heart raced. What if he told him to go home? What if Ivan didn't have a chance to try out his plan?

But instead, Jarmansky quietly closed the door. He walked to his window, and gazed for a few minutes at the busy Moscow street.

When he turned around, he was smiling slightly. Pointing to a chair, he invited Ivan to sit down.

"The *Pravda* idea is an interesting one, Comrade Nazaroff. I could have thought of it myself. Very interesting."

Ivan leaned slightly forward in his chair. He felt as if he were balancing on a tightrope. "It is too bad that Pyotr ran away from home, as you say. But if he *came* home, such a story would be possible."

Jarmansky was tapping the side of his desk, thoughtfully. "Perhaps you might know where young Pyotr is. Perhaps you might be able to persuade him to return home to his poor mother."

Ivan said nothing.

"It is important to this office that we counterattack false stories about the Soviet system of justice. Very important. If you could be helpful in this way, you would be doing your country a great service."

"Why is Mrs. Kachenko being brought to trial?" Ivan knew his question might anger the officer. He asked it as politely as possible.

But Jarmansky seemed indifferent to matters concerning her trial. He shrugged. "We have reason to believe she is an unfit mother. The trial will determine this."

Again Ivan spoke as politely as possible. "Forgive me, Comrade, but I am sure Mrs. Kachenko is a very good mother. I am sure the court will see this if she is brought to trial." Ivan paused. "If only she didn't have to be brought to trial."

There was silence in the room. Ivan knew Comrade Jarmansky was sizing him up. Finally he spoke. His voice was cool and deliberate.

"If you know where your friend is, I have ways of making you tell."

Ivan's heart suddenly lurched, but he

was prepared. He waited until his voice was steady before he answered. "If I knew, Comrade, and you detained me here, I should think people would know why and would move Pyotr very quickly so that any information I could give you would no longer be true."

Again there was silence in the room. This time Ivan spoke. "If only Mrs. Kachenko didn't have to be brought to trial," he repeated. "Then I am sure Pyotr would return home. Then perhaps a story could be written to prove he is not in a boarding school away from his mother. Such a story could be sent around the world, could it not?"

Ivan could see that Comrade Jarmansky was agitated. His voice was stiffly controlled. "All our *Pravda* stories are available to foreign newspapers. They can reprint anything they like. We hope that they will use many of our stories so that peoples of the world may receive a picture of Soviet life."

Ivan almost smiled. Even in Moscow, as far as he could tell, people were bored with *Pravda*. He didn't imagine anyone else in the world would want to read its stories.

"Such a story would be a fine thing." Ivan sighed. "Mrs. Kachenko is a good mother. If only she didn't have to be brought to trial."

Jarmansky crashed both fists on the top of his desk. "All right, Nazaroff. Let me tell you what I was just thinking. If young Pyotr returned to his mother, that would say something about the kind of woman she is, wouldn't it? That her son would return?"

Ivan felt himself lurch on the tightrope. He fought for inner balance as Jarmansky continued.

"If such a son returned home, and a story that he was with his mother appeared in our papers, I suppose that perhaps such a trial would not have to take place. Perhaps merely a warning from our office would be sufficient in such a case."

Ivan wet his lips in excitement. He looked steadily at Comrade Jarmansky. "No trial?"

Jarmansky's face flushed with anger. He shrugged. "Of course, who can say what a young boy like Kachenko will do? But if he is at home, and available to us for a newspaper story ... I can arrange it: no trial."

Ivan held on against the flood of joy that threatened his balance. "That would be good news for Mrs. Kachenko, Comrade. Let us hope he returns home."

There was a glint of unwilling admiration in Jarmansky's eyes. "I expect he will return home!" He spat out the words. "That would be useful to our office."

Ivan steadied himself, and took a deep breath. "But there is one thing more I have been thinking, Comrade."

◆Homecoming

Ivan couldn't remember ever seeing Momma so happy. Katya quickly caught her festive mood and the two of them were flying from the kitchen to the living room with plates and glasses in preparation for the welcome home party for Pyotr.

Even Poppa had bought a huge bunch of flowers wrapped in shiny cellophane for Mrs. Kachenko and a smaller bunch for little Sonya. He was chuckling in anticipation of their surprise as he stuck them into vases of water.

Delicious smells of food cooking wafted from the kitchen. Vegetables were scarce in the early spring, but Momma had found some onions for onion dumplings. And baking in the oven were rows of *piroshki*, the small, meat-filled rolls Ivan loved.

The hands of the clock seemed hardly

to move. Ivan paced around the living room in an agony of excitement. He had shined the samovar in preparation for the quantities of pale tea Momma said they would consume. He had polished his shoes, polished Poppa's good shoes, and pushed the carpet-sweeper over the living room rug. Still it was not time for Mrs. Kachenko and Sonya to arrive from their apartment.

Ivan tried to keep out of Momma's way. Every time she noticed him, she gave him another job. He went into the bedroom and sat down.

"Ivan! Ivan! What are you doing?" Momma's voice pulled him back into the living room. "Look at the time! Put the sour cream into a bowl and bring out some bottles of mineral water from the cupboard!"

Poppa grinned at Ivan. Poppa was unwrapping the family Bible he kept carefully folded in a copy of *Pravda*. Ivan knew Poppa would especially enjoy choosing the after-dinner Bible reading for tonight!

In the kitchen, Katya stopped shelling some eggs and looked anxiously at Ivan. "Are you sure the pastor will bring Pyotr at seven? What if they come too soon?" Ivan scraped out the paper carton of sour cream, trying to concentrate on Katya. "Pastor Aranovich went to get him. Of course he'll be here."

Katya's eyes shone. "To think that Mrs. Kachenko doesn't know anything! That Pyotr is coming home, that there is to be no trial! No wonder Poppa bought flowers!"

Momma rushed into the kitchen to check the *piroshki* in the tiny oven. "And you must not spoil the surprise, Katya," she warned as she pulled out the fragrant rolls. "Mrs. Kachenko thinks that she and Sonya are coming here only for dinner. Pyotr will arrive just a few minutes after his mother and Sonya. You can keep still a few minutes, Katya!"

"Yes, Momma." Katya returned to shelling the eggs with a great smile at Ivan.

"And don't look so happy!" Ivan warned. "Momma, Katya will spoil the surprise without saying one word. Make her stay in the kitchen."

Katya opened her mouth to protest, but Momma laughed. She gave Katya a playful tug at her braid. "She'll be all right."

There was a soft knocking at the door. Ivan's heart raced. He hoped Mrs. Kachenko didn't notice anything unusual as Poppa took her coat and Katya unzipped Sonya's little jacket. Ivan felt he might suddenly laugh at the change that had come over Momma. Her merriment had vanished. Quietly she led Mrs. Kachenko into the living room and sat with her on the sofa holding her hand as they chatted. Mrs. Kachenko looked very tired. She leaned back against the cushions. "It is kind of you to invite Sonya and me to dinner. Everything looks so pretty and smells so good. It's like a party." Katya, carrying Sonya around the room on her back, suddenly choked. Mrs. Kachenko looked concerned. "Katya, Sonya is too heavy for you. You shouldn't carry her."

"She's all right." Momma patted Mrs. Kachenko's arm.

Ivan tried desperately not to stare at the door. Poppa went back to turning the pages of the Bible. Katya began singing in an innocent voice. Momma and Mrs. Kachenko chatted on the sofa. The clock ticked loudly.

Finally there was knocking again at the door. Ivan rushed to throw it open. The

Nazaroffs' smiles of anticipation froze on their faces. Ivan backed into the room, trembling with emotion. Standing in the doorway was Pyotr's father, Mr. Kachenko. Beside him was Pyotr, smiling radiantly, and Pastor Aranovich, who pushed them into the room and quickly shut the door.

Mrs. Kachenko gave a terrible gasp. Ivan thought she might faint, but instead she rushed into her husband's arms. Poppa's face was drained of color. Momma began to cry, half in fear and half in joy. Sonya was a flash of yellow curls and flying ribbons as she hurled herself at her Poppa in joy.

Pastor Aranovich led them to the sofa and they sat down in a confusion of laughter and hugs and questions.

"But how are you here?" "Are you all right?" "You look so thin!" "You look so beautiful!" "What has happened?"

Finally Mr. Kachenko took his eyes away from his family and stood up to greet Poppa. The two men embraced without a word. Mr. Kachenko hugged Ivan a long time, then Katya. He sat down and embraced his own family all over again. Momma opened a drawer and gave a handkerchief to Mrs. Kachenko. She took out one for herself and wiped her eyes.

"Everybody sit down." Pastor Aranovich spoke softly, but Poppa put the small short-wave radio by the door and turned it on. Lovely music filled the air. The joyful sound was so fitting everyone smiled.

"I will try to be simple and I will try to begin at the beginning." Pastor Aranovich also wiped his eyes as he began to speak.

"The reason the authorities were insistent that you denounce your husband, Sister Kachenko, was that in his trial, it was written in the records that you *had* done this and had said your husband would not work and was a parasite on society."

Mrs. Kachenko flushed indignantly. "But I did not! I was not even given opportunity to speak."

The pastor nodded. "I know. Of course you did not. But it was because of this false testimony that he was sent to the prison camps."

Poppa leaned forward in his chair. "And when we appealed the case, you got to see the records, Brother Aranovich?"

"Yes. I understood why the government was determined to force our sister here to

lie about her husband."

Pyotr hugged his mother. "Dear Momma. We will have to let them put a picture of us in the paper. But there will be no trial."

Poppa cleared his throat. "Now, Ivan, is the part your Momma and I have been waiting for. All that you have said so far, we knew. Now you will explain how it is that our blessed brother Kachenko has returned. Truly, it is the Lord's doing. But it seems you also had a part." Poppa glanced at Pastor Aranovich who was grinning broadly in agreement.

The last moments in Comrade Jarmansky's office flashed into Ivan's mind. How different it had been then! How terrified he had been to go on with the conversation.

"What one thing more have you been thinking?" Jarmansky had growled. Ivan could see he didn't like bargains.

"As you have said, Comrade," Ivan had begun, "Pyotr Kachenko's return home would be useful to your office. Certainly his picture in the paper would prove wrong the part of the story about Pyotr. But there is much more in the story."

"That will be enough." Jarmansky had

shifted in his chair.

"Excuse me, Comrade, but I do not think so."

Jarmansky had shaken his head in exasperation. His great fat jowls wobbled under his chin. "We have talked enough, young Comrade."

Ivan had been silent.

"*Why* do you not think so?" Jarmansky's words burst out in open anger.

"I have heard, Comrade, that there is a document in existence."

"What sort of document?" Jarmansky was shouting. Ivan fought to keep his own voice calm. His knees trembled.

"A document from the trial, Comrade. Somebody could prove the newspaper statement about Pastor Kachenko's conviction on false evidence. Unless Pastor Kachenko himself is returned home, I think the document might be sent to the foreign papers. Then a story about Pyotr would not be enough."

"Get out! Get out! Get out!" Jarmansky's rage had been terrible.

He had moved much faster than Ivan would have thought possible. Pulling Ivan out of his chair, with a mighty heave he had thrown open the door and pushed Ivan through it. His hands and voice had been shaking with fury.

Poppa began laughing in delight. "But he knew you were telling the truth! He knew you were right!"

"I didn't know for sure what he was thinking," Ivan grinned. "I only knew I was glad to be out of his office and walking down the street."

Momma's eyes were full of tears. "And you didn't tell us about this part!"

"Because I didn't know what he would do. I thought I had only made him more angry."

Pyotr got up from his father's side on the couch and moved toward Ivan. Momma clapped her hands. "We must eat!"

She hurried into the kitchen, calling Katya after her. Poppa and Pastor Aranovich began pouring tea, watching the steam rise from the samovar like prayers. Mrs. Kachenko was weeping with joy, her head on her husband's shoulder, Sonya on her lap.

The two boys stood looking at one another. "Ivan," Pyotr's voice was husky. He embraced his friend and then stood back with a grin. "Thanks to God. Thanks to you."

Ivan gave Pyotr a playful push. "Come on, Pyotr. Let's have dinner. Then I'll race you to the Moscow River! All the ice is melted now!"